D1399592

Cade's Redemption
(The Western Adventures of
Cade McCall III)

by

Robert Vaughan

WOLFPACK
PUBLISHING
— EST 2013 —

Print Edition
© Copyright 2017 Robert Vaughan

Wolfpack Publishing
P.O. Box 620427
Las Vegas, NV 89162

ISBN: 978-1-62918-675-7

Cade's Redemption

By

Robert Vaughan

Prologue

Twin Creek Ranch, Howard County, Texas – 1927:

CADE MCCALL had pinned a target to a large oak tree and he and Owen Wister were standing thirty feet from it. Owen grasped a knife by its point, then threw it at the target. It hit handle-first, bounced off the tree, then stuck up in the ground just below the target.

"Well at least I hit the target," Owen said.

"Yeah, and you might have even given him a bruise," Cade teased as he raised his own knife for the toss. Whipping his hand forward, the knife rotated once, then hit the target, stabbing almost an inch deep into the tree. "Now, that would have stopped him."

"I'll say it would." Owen walked up to the tree to retrieve the two knives.

Owen Wister, well known as the author of *The Virginian*, among other stories, had come to Twin Creek Ranch, Cade McCall's 60,000 acre cattle ranch in Central Texas, to interview the man about whom more than a few books had been written. Because of his storied past, he had been portrayed on the movie screen by such actors as Gary Cooper and William S. Hart.

Wister was here because he planned to write the definitive biography, *The Western Adventures of Cade McCall, His Story, As told to Owen Wister.*

"Are you ready to get to work?" Wister asked.

"Yes."

"So, where do we start?"

Cade was silent for a long moment. "We start from a very dark place."

Chapter One

CADE MCCALL WAS sitting at a poker table—what bar it was he didn't know and he didn't care. Hell, he didn't even know what town he was in, but it didn't matter. For the last year he had tried to put behind him all that he knew and a bottle of whiskey had been the best helper. Lifting his empty glass, he turned to the girl who was hovering around the table.

"Another one," Cade said slurring his words. "Get me another one."

"Honey, don't you want to slow down a bit?" the attractive woman asked as she patted Cade's shoulder. "You're way ahead of everybody else."

Cade laughed. "I think you got that wrong." He tapped the chips in front of him that indicated he had been having a run of bad luck.

"Dammit, Lola, get the man a drink," one of the men at the table said. "And get your hands off this skunk. If you're gonna be sharin' my bed, I don't want his stink to rub off on you."

Lola glared at the man as she turned toward the bar.

"What's it gonna be, McCall? Are you in or out?"

Cade studied his hand.

"The bet on the table is a hundred and fifty," the man said.

What had started as a regular card game had progressed rapidly into a high-dollar game, the increased cost of playing sustained by Luke Slater, who was literally buying the pots by his excessive bets. Now only Cade and Slater were still in the game.

Cade was holding an ace-over full house, and he was certain it was a winner.

"Get me something to write on," Cade called to the bartender.

When Lola returned with the drink, she had a pen, an ink bottle and a slip of paper.

Downing the drink in one gulp, Cade picked up the pen, dipped it in the ink, and wrote something on the paper.

"I'll see your bet and raise it a hundred," Cade said as he shoved the paper into the middle of the table.

Slater started to rake in the pot. "Game's over McCall."

Cade grabbed Slater's hand. "Look at the paper." He held up his cards. "I've got a winning hand here and . . ."

That was as far as he got before there was the sound of a gunshot in his ear, and the cards he was holding flew out of his hand.

"You son of a bitch!" Cade shouted as he turned to punch the man behind him who had pulled the trigger.

When Cade McCall awoke the next morning, he was aware of two things. His left eye was swollen shut, and he was in jail.

Groaning, he put his hand to the swollen eye, then because it was sensitive to the touch, he jerked it back, quickly.

"Hurts, don't it?" someone said, with a little chuckle.

"Where am I?" Cade asked.

"You're in the cooler, that's where you're at."

"I know I'm jail."

Cade's cell mate laughed again. "How long you been drunk?"

"About a year, I guess."

"Well, sir, you're in Caldwell. That's Kansas," he added, "in case you don't even know what state you're in."

"Did I kill somebody?"

"You might have. It happens pretty regular around here. All's I know is you was fit to be tied when they dragged you in here. Why, the constable had to give you a whack on your head to get you settled down."

Cade sat up, and felt a lump on the back of his head. When he did he experienced a sudden dizziness that caused a wave of nausea.

"If you're 'bout to throw up, use the piss pot," the other prisoner said.

Cade grabbed the pot, and the smell of urine brought on instant regurgitation. He threw up in the pot, then set it down.

"That whiskey don't taste near as good comin' out as it did goin' in, do it?"

Cade glared at the man as he wiped his mouth with the back of his hand.

The door that separated the cells from the rest of the jail house opened, and someone came in.

"Well, good, I'm glad you're alive," the constable said. "Me and Slim here were thinkin' you'd be out all day."

"Slim?"

"That would be me. Slim Cooley." The man in the cell offered Cade his hand. "Glad to meet you. I didn't get your name."

"It doesn't matter," Cade said.

"Oh, my. He's a bad one," the constable said. "Too good for the likes of Caldwell."

Cade cocked his eyebrow as he looked toward the constable.

"You could tell me why I'm here."

"Ask Dusty Coleman. You got into a fight and pretty much tore the Pig Lot apart."

"The pig lot? I know I was playing cards and that I got into a tussle but how did I tear up a pig lot?"

"You really have been drunk for a year, ain't ya? The Pig Lot's a saloon," Slim said.

"Oh." Cade put his hands to his head and looked down.

"I don't suppose you want anything to eat," the constable said, "but when you want somethin', you just tell me. Slim here can tell you, I make a mighty fine pot of beans and a good corn pone."

"When can I get out of here?" Cade asked.

"That all depends. Dusty said you owe him about three hundred dollars, and from what I found in your pockets, I'd say you'll be here about six months."

"Six months?"

The constable nodded his head. "It ain't so bad, but then if you don't behave, we can send you to Wellington. Now, over there, they don't much cotton to your kind."

"You said I was in a fight. I don't think Slim's the one I was fighting with, but I don't see anybody else in jail. Why is it I'm the one who has to pay?"

"Oh, there was enough damage to go around. But the Slaters ponied up the money to pay their part."

"The Slaters?"

"Yeah. Dusty said you was in a game with Luke Slater, and you didn't like the way it was goin' so you took after his brother. Now, them Slater boys stick together. When you fight one of 'em, you fight all three."

"I see," Cade said.

"Now do you want some beans?" the constable asked.

"I'd like to send a telegram."

"How you gonna do that, when I know you ain't got two nickels to rub together?"

"I'll send it collect," Cade said.

"Wake up."

Luke Slater groaned.

"Wake up," the woman said as she applied a damp cloth to the man's swollen lip.

"I'm awake, I'm awake," Luke said.

Opening his eyes, he saw Lola Fontaine sitting on the side of the bed.

"You're dressed."

"That's what people do when it's after noon," Lola said continuing to wipe his face.

"Did I give you a good time?"

7

"If you call cleaning up after a fight a good time, then yes, I had an extra good time. You owe me, and you owe me a lot."

"If we didn't do anything, then I don't owe you anything."

"It's the Pig Lot," Lola said. "Dusty sent Leonard to Wichita this morning for lumber, but it'll take at least a month before the saloon's back to the way it was."

Slater tried to laugh, but his lip was too sore to allow it.

"You're a good woman, Lola. Who knows, I might want to marry you, some day."

"No, Luke, I don't think so. I'm not going to marry anyone who knows I was a whore. When I get enough money put aside, I'm heading east. I'll find me some decent man, tell him I'm a widow, and settle down and raise a houseful of kids."

"I don't believe it. Where on earth could you find a better life than this?"

"Humph. You don't really know me, Luke Slater. Any one of us would give an eye tooth to be the wife of some farmer or storekeeper or whatever job he had. We don't whore because we want to."

"But you like it," Luke said as he got out of bed and padded across the room where his hat lay on the chest of drawers. He put his hat on, then turned toward Lola.

"Now, don't go anywhere. I'll be back." He started toward the door, and Lola laughed.

"What's so funny?"

"Don't you think you might want to wear more than just your hat?"

Luke looked down at himself. "Oh, I reckon I better."

When Luke came down the stairs, he felt his jaw as he surveyed the Pig Lot. Lola was right. It would take a while before the saloon was fixed up. He had to wonder how one man could have done that much damage. As far as he could remember, no one had taken McCall's side while the fight was going on. As for him, he knew his brothers had whipped the man in a fair fight—that is if you called three against one a fair fight.

When he got out on the street, he saw his brother, Mack, leaning against the hitching rail, two horses standing at the ready.

"Where's Weasel?" Luke asked.

"He's down at the dugout," Mack said pulling out his watch. "I was gonna give you another ten minutes and then I was gonna come drag you out of that whore's bed."

"Well, now, you should have done that. I would have shared."

"Let's get out of here. We've spent too much time in Sumner County already. We can't keep those horses down below the bluff forever."

"That's why we've got the Nations. An Indian will take any horse he can get, and be happy."

"True, but we've got to get them there first. Let's hope Sheriff Ross isn't out looking for old O'Bannon's horses."

"Is that all we've got?" Luke asked. "We didn't get more'n a half dozen from that old man."

"No, stupid. That's not all we have, but Weasel can't hide thirty horses all by himself."

Of the three brothers, Luke was the oldest, and Weasel was the youngest. Despite the fact that Mack was in the middle, he had assumed the leadership role, and neither Luke nor Weasel challenged him.

Chapter Two

THE CONSTABLE ENTERED the room and unlocked the door to the cell where Cade had been incarcerated for six days.

"Let's go."

Slim Cooley rose to his feet, a wide smile on his face. "This ain't been too bad. I'll miss your cookin'."

"It ain't you, Slim. It this here other'n."

"I thought you said I'd be here six months," Cade said rising from his bunk.

"That fella you sent the telegram to must've thought you were worth the money. He paid the damages, so I don't have no reason to hold you no longer. Why, if I had to keep ever cowboy who started a fight, I'd have to have a jail bigger'n the hotel."

When Cade followed the constable into the front of the jail house, he saw Jeter Willis leaning against one of the two desks. He had his arms folded across his chest, and the expression on his face was one of disapproval.

Cade nodded his head toward Jeter, as the constable handed him his gun and holster.

"Do me a favor, will you McCall?" the constable asked. "If you're going to bust up another saloon, would you consider doing it somewhere else?"

"Where's my hat?" Cade asked.

"It didn't come with ya when you was brought in the other night. If I was a bettin' man, I'd say it's half way to Wichita on some drover's head if it was any good."

"Let's get out of here," Cade said as he headed for the door.

"I should have left you there," Jeter said when the two men were out on the street.

"Please, Jeter, no lecture. There's nothing you can say to me that I haven't already said to myself."

"I took a room at the hotel," Jeter said. "We'll start back first thing tomorrow morning. In the meantime, you need a bath and a haircut."

"Yeah," Cade said. "I'm so ripe I can smell myself."

It was a much cleaner and better smelling Cade McCall who walked into the Palace Café for dinner that evening. Though the swelling had gone down, there was still some discoloration around Cade's left eye as he took his seat across the table from Jeter.

"You want to tell me about it?" Jeter asked, after they ordered their meal.

"Tell you about what?"

"About what in the hell gave you the idea that you could take on three men without getting your ass whipped."

"To be honest, Jeter, I was too drunk to even remember the fight. But I can't believe that I was drunk enough to try and take on three men."

"They're brothers," Jeter said. "And from what I've been able to find out, they're regular hellions. When I paid for the damages, the barkeep told me you'd come closer to whipping the Slaters than anyone else has, and that he and several others were hoping that you would." Jeter chuckled. "Apparently you left the three of them pretty bruised up."

Cade smiled as he fingered the cut under his eye. "I'm glad it wasn't all one-sided."

"When are you goin' to come home 'n quit this nonsense, Cade?"

"Humph. Where would that be? Tennessee? Galveston? Just where is home?"

"You know where home is. Home is where your daughter is."

Cade's face hardened. "I don't have a daughter."

"Oh? I want you to look into the eyes of that little girl and tell her she's not your daughter."

"I don't have a daughter," Cade repeated.

"I don't know what's happened to you, Cade. You aren't the Cade I used to know, and I'd like for that Cade to come back."

"The Cade that you knew is no more."

"If I really thought that was true, I would've left you in jail."

"That's what you should have done," Cade said in a remorseful, self-condemning voice.

That night, Cade lay in bed in the hotel room staring up into the darkness. He hadn't had a drink for six days and without the alcohol induced fog, he was forced to face the memories that he couldn't make go away. He listened to the loud snores coming from Jeter, thinking how many times he had heard those sonorous tones before.

It had been two and a half years ago when Cade and Jeter brought up a herd of cattle from Southeast Texas to Abilene, Kansas. He had to smile when he thought about the excitement they had felt when the McCall and Willis Cattle Company got the contract from Linus Puckett to take charge of a combined herd.

And then there was the chuck wagon. At the last moment, the cook they had hired was thrown in jail, and Arabella DuPree, the woman he loved, volunteered to come along on the drive as the cook.

Cade had protested, saying a cattle drive was no place for a woman, but Arabella had persisted. In the end, she convinced him that she and her friend, Magnolia, would be the best cooks any cattle drive would ever have. Finally, he succumbed to her reasoning, but insisted that she could only come with them if she came as his wife.

Arabella had been right. No cattle drive had ever eaten food quite like that prepared for the McCall and Willis Company, and thinking back upon those few months Cade knew it had been the happiest time of his life. But then because of one disastrous error in judgement on his part, all that had changed. As the herd was coming through Wichita, Cade sent the chuck wagon on ahead without any escort. When he caught up with the wagon, it looked as if there had been a terrible accident, but Arabella and Magnolia were nowhere to be found. And then he knew. The lead mule had been shot in the head. Arabella and Magnolia had been kidnapped.

He searched for his wife for an entire year, first on his own, and then as a civilian scout assigned to the Eleventh Cavalry at Fort Dodge. It was during the time he was a scout that he discovered the women had not been taken by Indians as he had believed, but were taken by Amon Kilgore, a man who had been a competing trail boss from Texas. When he learned that Kilgore and his partner were buffalo hunters, he became a driver for a freight wagon traveling between Fort Dodge and Camp Supply knowing that someday he would run across someone who knew where the bastards were. He vowed he would find them and kill them.

He pressed his search, following false leads, running up blind trails, frustrated by failure after failure. In all that time, he never abandoned the hunt and never gave up hope, because he was obsessed with finding his wife. Then the search ended suddenly, and unexpectedly, when he stopped for provisions at Dunnigan's Goods on the Bent Canyon Road.

That was when he saw Magnolia, nursing a child.

And he found Arabella.

Mr. Dunnigan led Cade to a room in the back of the store where he saw his wife lying in a pool of blood. He heard the cry of a baby, as Mrs. Dunnigan began to swaddle a child. At first Cade was filled with pride at the thought of becoming a father, but that pride soon changed to anger. What had his wife endured at the hands of Amon Kilgore?

Distraught by the knowledge that Arabella had been violated, he swore he would love her so much that she would forget anything that had happened to her. He knelt by her bed, and she turned toward him, her hand reaching out to touch his face. She rubbed her fingers over his lips.

"Cade, promise me you'll take care of her."

"We will. We'll do it together."

"I won't be here. You'll have to…"

Those were the last words he had heard from his dying wife.

Shortly thereafter, Jeter married Maggie, and announced that he was going to open a saloon in Dodge City.

Cade became Jeter's silent partner, putting up half the money needed to build the saloon, but he had other things on his mind. He was determined to find the two men and bring them to justice . . . not in a court of law, but in his own, private court of justice.

After six months of searching, he found them at a place on King Fisher Creek in the Nations, where they were, illegally, selling whiskey to the Indians. He made a positive identification, by binoculars, of the two men; Amon Kilgore and Fred Toombs.

For a moment, Cade considered confronting them. Part of him wanted them to know who killed them, and why. Then he decided they didn't deserve to be faced down. He had killed men during the war, good men, sons, husbands, and fathers, for no reason other than that they were wearing a different color uniform. If he could kill good men from afar, he could kill these two sons of bitches.

He made two head shots from five hundred yards away with his Sharps Fifty, and left them where they fell. There was no need to check on them, he knew they were dead.

***

Cade jumped out of bed drenched in sweat. Nothing in his entire life had affected him the way Arabella's death had done—not hiding under a mound of dying men at the battle of Franklin, not surviving a year in a Yankee prison camp, not escaping a tyrant in Argentina, not even killing Kilgore and Toombs. All of those actions were meaningless, when they were compared to the anguish he felt as he watched the flicker of life fade from Arabella's eyes.

Cade had to get out of this room. He needed a drink.

Cade and Jeter were camped on Soldier's Creek two days into what would be a four-day trip back to Buffalo City. Jeter brought out the last of the biscuits he had brought with them from Caldwell.

"We'll have to do some huntin' tomorrow," he said, handing a piece of ham to Cade.

"It shouldn't be too hard to bag a prairie chicken or a jack rabbit," Cade said as he grabbed the coffee pot. "Damn, that thing's hot." He drew back his hand quickly.

The two men sat around the fire until Jeter finally broke the silence.

"What are you going to do when you get back?"

"I don't know. Maybe I can get a job at one of the saloons, or maybe I'll just keep playing poker for a living. You know, I'm pretty good."

"You don't have to do that. If you're going to work at a saloon, why don't you work at the one you own?"

"It doesn't belong to me," Cade said. "You and Magnolia are the ones who have built up the business."

"The hell it doesn't," Jeter said. "The Red House Saloon belongs to you just as much as it belongs to me. We sold the ranch and the money we made from the cattle drive paid for the place. I could use your help. With the railroad coming I expect the town will grow, and our business will double. And besides that, Magnolia needs to stay home with the girls."

"Your ma's not there anymore?"

"Of course she is, but she was stoved up before I brought her up from Texas. And with Bella and Chantal growing like weeds, she can't keep up with them."

"Are they walkin'?"

"Chantal is. If you came around more, you'd see how cute they are together. Both have black hair and big black eyes just like their mothers. When people see 'em everybody thinks they're twins."

"That's good. Magnolia's a fine mother."

"She is. You know, she lost our baby a couple months back. Nearly killed her."

Cade jerked his head up.

"No, no. I didn't mean to say that, Cade. It wasn't like Arabella. She wants another baby—our baby and it just hasn't happened yet. But it will."

Cade took a deep breath. "What about Pete Cahill? Is he still working for you?"

Jeter smiled. "Checkin' up on your investment, are you? I thought you didn't care what happened to The Red House."

Cade shrugged his shoulders. "It doesn't matter to me, just as long as you make enough to keep your family together."

"And that we make enough to keep bailing you out of jail," Jeter added. "When is all this carousing gonna stop? You need to think about what you're doing with your life."

"No, I don't," Cade said. He walked over to the fire and, using his hat as a heat pad this time, picked up the coffee pot and poured himself a cup. "It's better when I don't think about anything at all."

"You can't go the rest of your life like this, Cade."

"Why not?"

"You just can't. You're a young man, barely thirty years old, and you need a woman—a wife, like I've got Magnolia. Do you think I don't know the hell she's put up with? First New Orleans, when it was Arabella who showed her a way to get out, and then those bastards, what they did to her. But we've put all that behind us, and you could do the same thing," Jeter insisted.

"You think I don't want to?" Cade asked. He took a swallow of his coffee as he composed his thoughts. "More than anything in the world, I want to put Arabella's death behind me. But I can't get that awful image out of my mind. Whether my eyes are open or closed, all I can see is Arabella, lying in that pool of blood, her life slipping away before me. And I was helpless . . . helpless to do anything!" Cade threw the tin cup into the bushes as he kicked at the fire.

"I shouldn't have brought this up," Jeter said. "I just made it worse."

"You didn't make it worse," Cade said, shaking his head. "Nothing could make it worse than it already is."

Ten miles north and west of where Cade and Jeter were camped, a small band of Indians was watching the house of a homesteader. Waquini, a self-proclaimed medicine man from the Kiowa-Comanche Reservation, waited with four warriors who had agreed to follow him. Translated into English, his name meant One with Hooked Nose, the name given him when, as a child, he had fallen and broken his nose.

Waquini had taken it upon himself to punish the White Man for the wrongs they had done the Indians, and if it meant leaving Indian Territory and coming into Kansas, so be it. He and his followers had reached the farmhouse just before dawn. Now the sun was up, and they could smell the rich aromas of bacon and coffee.

"I think we will eat well this morning," Waquini said.

"I hope the woman has made much bacon," Keytano said.

"Quiet, the man comes," Waquini cautioned.

Waquini and the others saw a man walk toward the small house where the Whites did their toilet. They watched him as he went inside, then waited for a short time. When he came back outside, he was hooking his suspenders over his shoulders.

Waquini drew back the bow then released the arrow. It flew true, the shaft burying the arrow head deep into the man's chest.

With the man down, Waquini and the others charged the house. The woman looked up shocked and terrified by the sudden and unexpected appearance of Indians in her kitchen. She screamed just as she was knocked to the floor.

"Ma!" a shout came from the sleeping loft, and a boy, about twelve dropped to the kitchen. He grabbed a butcher knife and ran at one of the Indians, but Waquini killed him with the same war club he had used to kill the boy's mother

"The boy was brave," Waquini acknowledged as he grabbed a biscuit.

"There's no need to hunt today," Cade said when he and Jeter were striking their camp the next morning. "We should be passing the Johansson place around noon."

"They're good people, Halen and his wife," Jeter said. He laughed. "Do you think she'll have a pot of rabbit and dumplin' stew going?"

"Don't Swedes call that klimp?" Cade asked.

"I don't know what she calls it but it sure was good the last time I was out this way."

The two men rode in relative silence for the rest of the morning until Cade saw the buzzards.

"Cade?" The tone of Jeter's voice made it obvious that he had seen them as well. "Could that be…?"

"The Johansson place, yes," Cade said, answering the question before it was asked. "Come on!"

Cade slapped his legs against the side of his horse, urging it into a gallop. Jeter was right behind him.

When they reached the farm, Cade saw the buzzards. Pulling his pistol, he fired a couple of shots into the air and a dozen or more birds took to the sky, leaving a bloody body on the ground.

Cade dismounted and hurried to find a body where he saw an arrow shaft sticking from the chest.

"Is it Halen?" Jeter asked.

"There's hardly enough left to identify, but I'm sure it is," Cade said. The body had been scalped, stripped, and mutilated.

With pistols drawn, the two men went into the house. Cade was saddened, but not surprised by what he found. Astrid Johansson and her son were lying on the floor, their bodies only slightly less desecrated than Halen's had been.

"Do you think this was done by Indians, or was it those damn bastards who are roaming the country stealing horses, making it look like it's Indians?" Jeter asked.

"Either way, these people need to be buried," Cade said. "I'll find a shovel."

Chapter Three

WHEN CADE AND JETER rode into town Cade was amazed to see all the activity, as frame buildings were going up on every street. These were replacing the tents that had been thrown up when the military had expanded Fort Dodge, forcing the closing of the settlement that had grown up across the Arkansas River.

"What's happening to Buffalo City?" Cade asked.

"Mainly, the railroad," Jeter answered. "And it's not Buffalo City any more. The railroad wants it called Dodge City, so that's what it's going to be."

"Tell that to the buffalo hunters." They passed by a large, fenced-in lot, in which were stacked thousands of dried buffalo hides. Cade read the sign. "Rath and Company. Would that be Charlie Rath?"

"Yes, and the 'company' is Bob Wright. He's still out at the sutler's store, but he thinks thinks he can make more money in Dodge City," Jeter said.

Cade began counting the saloons along the main thoroughfare. "It looks like your saloon has a lot of competition," he said.

"Everybody wants to be close to the railroad. That is, if it ever gets here."

"I think I heard the track's already been laid west of Larned," Cade said. "If ever there was easy track laying it's going through Kansas."

"Geography's not the problem. It's horse thieves," Jeter said.

"Indian raids?"

"I suppose some of it's done by Indians, but most of the stealing's done by whites. The military went after the bunch that took close to a hundred head when they were laying track up by Hutchinson."

"Did they catch 'em?" Cade asked.

"Sure did. The herder disappeared the same night the horses did, so the Army pretty much knew who they were going after. But the forty horses that were taken from the graders a week or so back—nobody knows who did that. They're long gone."

"We should tell the army what we found out at the Johansson's," Cade said.

"I'll let Bob Wright know. He'll tell Colonel Dodge about the raid," Jeter said. "I expect the army will send out a patrol."

"I hope they find whoever did this, whether they be Indian or whites."

"They might find who did it, but I wouldn't count on it. If it is Indians, it's generally just a few out on their own, to cause trouble, and if it's whites, they run the stock out of here as fast as they can."

Jeter reined his horse in and stopped. "I'm going this way, Cade. Why don't you come with me? I've put up a house over on Walnut and we can make room for you to stay there. And besides that you'd see Magnolia and the girls."

"No."

"Cade, I really think you should."

"No," Cade repeated, more forcefully.

"All right, I sure as hell can't force you to come, even though you do have a responsibility toward Chantal."

"Is Magnolia not getting enough money out of the saloon to look after her? Or do I need to pay you more?"

"That's a hell of thing to say," Jeter said, his voice clearly showing his disgust. "You damn well know it's not about money."

"Jeter I...I just can't," Cade replied, as he looked away, not wanting to face his friend.

With a resigned sigh, Jeter answered. "If that's how you want it."

"That's what I want."

Jeter extended his hand to Cade with a twenty-dollar bill in it. "I thought you might need this."

"I don't need your money, Jeter. I'll be just fine."

"It's not my money, it's your money. Anyway, how do you expect to finance your first hand of poker?"

Cade took the money, then the two men separated. Jeter turned to go to his house and his wife, and Cade rode down to the end of Front Street. He was surprised to see a new hotel called The Essington House. He walked in to inquire for a place to stay.

"Yes, sir," the clerk said, "we've got a room for you. It just got the roof put on yesterday."

"A roof's a good thing to have," Cade said, as he signed the book.

"How long will you be staying...Mr. McCall?" the clerk asked reading the name upside down.

"I don't know."

"Well, sir, I'll have to have the money now. New people are flocking into Buffalo—I mean Dodge City—every day. And you can see we can't get lumber fast enough to build more rooms. Everybody's waiting for the railroad."

"All right, how much?" Cade took out the bill Jeter had just given him.

"It'll be a dollar a day."

"Mark me down for three days. I'll let you know how much longer I'll be here."

Cade went up to his room. The walls were covered with tar paper and the floor was bare boards, but the bed was clean and it looked comfortable. Smelling meat being cooked, he walked over to the window. He looked down at a tent which must have been serving as a kitchen for the restaurant he had seen to the left of the clerk's desk.

And then he saw it. A house not two blocks distant.

He knew without a doubt, this was Jeter's house. A white house with a red door and red shutters.

The Red House had been a boarding house in Galveston that Arabella had opened after she had left New Orleans. She bought it with money she had stolen from Cade, and when he had tracked her down, she had given him half ownership in the business.

That was the start of his infatuation with Arabella DuPree, the most beautiful woman he had ever seen.

Jeter had named the saloon they had bought together The Red House to honor the original building bearing that name, and hearing those words and seeing this house, so clearly meant to recall earlier times, brought back painful memories.

As he was watching, Cade saw Jeter stable his horse in an outbuilding behind his house. The red door opened and a slender woman with black hair came running out to meet him. She threw herself into his arms, and arm in arm he watched them go through the door and close it behind them.

A feeling of melancholy came over Cade. What made him think he could come back here? He had to ride on. Maybe Colorado, maybe Texas, maybe New Mexico. He didn't much care where it was, but the first order of business would be to make some money.

Chapter Four

THE RED HOUSE, one of only a handful of saloons that was a frame building, was crowded with men even though it was 10:00 a.m. There were buffalo hunters, bullwhackers, muleskinners, track layers and soldiers all mingling together, either standing at the bar or sitting at one of the tables playing a game of chance. Oliver Frost was running a game of chuck-a-luck, while Pete Cahill was tending bar. All seemed to be running smoothly and money was flowing into the coffers.

"Boss," Cahill said when Jeter entered the bar. "Heard you got back yesterday."

"I should have stopped by, but I knew you could handle it. Anything happen while I was gone?"

"Not much. Three more saloons opened and there was a killin' yesterday," Cahill said.

"Not here, I hope," Jeter said as he stepped behind the bar and retrieved an apron.

"No, it was over at Fat Tom's."

"Was it anybody we know?"

"No. Some track worker got a little rowdy and a bullwhacker took him out."

Jeter shook his head. "Something's got to be done about all this killing."

"And that's what I've come to talk about," a man said as he stepped up to the bar, extending his hand.

"Morning, Charlie," Jeter said. "What will you have?"

Everybody knew Charles Rath. He had moved West in the fifties as a young man, eventually becoming the leading trader with the Indians and buffalo hunters, as well as establishing a flourishing general store. And now he had established his business in Dodge where he was stockpiling buffalo hides awaiting the arrival of the railroad.

"I'll have a beer," Rath said. "I stopped by to see you a couple of days ago, but Pete told me you were out of town."

"That's right," Jeter said without further explanation.

"The talk is you had to go down to Caldwell and bail McCall out of jail again."

"Who told you that?"

"I don't know but that's what all the wags are saying. You should have left him in jail."

"I couldn't do that. He's my friend, and he's my business partner."

"What kind of partner is he? He's never here, and when he is around, he's usually three sheets to the wind," Charles said. He took a swallow of his beer. "At one time, I thought he was a good man, but when that wife of his died, it changed him. If you ask me, McCall's as worthless as tits on a boar hog, and you'd be a hell of a lot better off if you just shucked him."

"I didn't ask you."

Jeter moved down the bar to get another drink for a customer. When he returned, Charles was still sitting there, his glass empty.

"I came in here because tomorrow morning most of the businessmen are meeting over at Fringer's Apothecary, and you might want to come join us."

"What's it about?"

"The killings."

Jeter nodded his head. "Pete said it was at the dance hall."

"The last one was. The day before that it happened at the Alhambra. And no more 'n two weeks ago we had a shootout right out there in the middle of the street."

"I was here for that one," Jeter said. "For a town of less than 500 people, how many killings have we had this year already?"

"I haven't been here all year, but if you walk up on Boot Hill, you can count at least ten or fifteen new graves," Charles said. "We've got to get some law and order in this place, or someone who's dear to us is gonna be next. I'm bringin' my wife out when the train gets here, and I want it to be safe for her to walk our streets."

"I agree. What time did you say the meeting would start?" Jeter asked.

"Henry says to come about eleven. All of you who work nights should be up by then."

The next morning while all the leading business owners were gathering at the apothecary for their meeting, Cade McCall was in The Alhambra Saloon, playing poker with Dooley Coulter, Ian Bligh, and Cap Jensen. Coulter and Bligh worked as hostlers and mechanics for the Southern Kansas Stage Line. Nobody quite knew the source of Jensen's income, but he never seemed to be without money. It was rumored, though there was no actual way of substantiating it, that Jensen had robbed a bank down in Texas. He was, if anyone had been pressed to quantify him, a genuine desperado who had already been in two shooting scrapes in Dodge City alone, and it was rumored that he had killed at least three men. He was not a man anyone wanted to cross.

"Hey, Cade, how come you're not at the meetin' this mornin'?" Coulter asked."

"What meeting?" Cade asked as he picked up the cards from the latest deal.

"They's some kind of a meetin' a' goin' on down at the drug store. All I know about it is that it's for all the businessmen in town."

"I'm not a businessman," Cade said.

"You own half the Red House, don't you?"

"I don't have anything to do with it. That's Jeter's operation."

"But the way he tells it, you own half of it. That's makes you a businessman," Bligh said. "Leastwise, in my book it does."

Cade laughed. "Are you inviting me to the meeting, Mr. Bligh?"

"What? Hell no, I can't do nothin' like that."

"Well, there you are. Mr. Bligh would invite me to the meeting, but he doesn't have the authority. And those who have it are disinclined to include me." Cade lifted his glass, in salute to the table, then downed the whiskey.

"I thought we was here to play cards," Jensen said.

"Well, just what is it you think we're a' doin', if we ain't a playin' cards?" Coulter asked.

"Seems to me like all youse is doin' is jawbonin'," Jensen said. "You got a jack high showin', Bligh. It's your bet."

Down at the opposite end of Front Street the Fringer Apothecary was closed for business. The leading citizens of the town were meeting, with Robert Wright conducting the proceedings.

"As all of you know, we had yet another killing here, yesterday. That's the sixteenth killing this year."

"Damn. That many. It's almost like we're back in the War again," A. B. Webster said.

"Eb Collar's not complaining. Hell, he's doin' more business than any of us," Moses Waters said with a laugh.

"Mr. Waters, an undertaker likes to be paid for his services," Collar said. "When these fellas die with nothing, the most I can do is wrap a sheet around 'em and make sure we plant 'em deep enough so the wolves won't get 'em."

"Next thing you know, old Collar'll be startin' a cobbler's shop." Webster chuckled when he thought of his own joke. "The sign'll say slightly used boots."

"Back to the purpose of this meeting," Wright continued. "I took it upon myself to write to Governor Harvey to see if the state could help us rein in this lawlessness. He said until we are incorporated we can't have any local law enforcement, and there's no sheriff for Ford County—in fact, all of Southwest Kansas. We've got the military, but we all know they only go after Indians or horse thieves so we can't count on their help. That leaves us with only one option." Wright stopped and looked around the room to make certain he had everyone's attention. "Gentlemen, we are about to incorporate the town of Dodge City."

"Dodge City?" Moses Waters asked. "What's wrong with Buffalo City? I have a hell of a lot more buffalo hunters in my place than I got soldiers from Fort Dodge."

"The railroad wants to call the town Dodge City," Daniel Wolfe said.

"Look, I want the railroad here as much as anyone else," Waters said. "But that don't mean they can start runnin' our town. What right do they have to tell us what to name this place? I still say we should call it Buffalo City."

"There's another problem with that, Moses, and it doesn't have anything to do with the railroad," Wright said. "It turns out there's already an incorporated town in Kansas called Buffalo, and the U.S. Mail won't allow us to use the same name."

"Well why didn't you say that in the first place? I can understand givin' in to the post office a lot better than rollin' over 'n playin' dead for the railroad."

"Hell, I got no problem with callin' it Dodge City," George Hoover said.

"Good, that saves some rewriting," Wright said.

"What rewriting? You mean it's already been written?" Waters asked.

"Yes."

"If it's already been written, what's the purpose of this here meeting?"

"Merely writing it doesn't ratify it," Wright said. "For that, we'll need half the people who live here to agree. Now, I'm going to read it to you, then I want all of you to sign it. After that we'll get a few more signatures, then submit it to the state capitol in Topeka…and the town of Dodge City will be in business."

"You mean with a mayor and a marshal and everything?" Hoover asked.

"Eventually. But to get it started, there will be a board of directors with seven directors."

"Who will the seven be?" Frederick Zimmerman asked.

"That's what we'll decide today. Charles, you drafted the charter, would you like to read it to us?"

Charles Rath walked up to the front of the room, cleared his throat, and began to read.

"Charter of the Dodge City Town Company, of Ford County, State of Kansas," he began.

"Be it remembered that on this, the 15th day of August, 1872…"

Chapter Five

AT THE OPPOSITE end of Front Street from the apothecary, Cade McCall was at The Alhambra, still absorbed in the card game that had occupied his time for most of the morning.

"Are you just goin' to sit there, McCall, or are you goin' to play cards?" Cap Jensen asked with a growl.

"What's your hurry, Jensen?" Coulter asked. "We all got a right to study our hand a bit."

"McCall's been studyin' it long enough," Jensen said.

"You're just upset that he's beatin' you is all," Coulter said.

"I fold," Cade said, laying his cards, face down.

"You fold? You son of a bitch, you're into me for almost a hunnert dollars!" Jensen said, angrily. "Now that I got me some good cards and a chance to get some of it back, you won't even play the hand?"

Cade picked up his whiskey glass and tossed the rest of his drink down before holding it up to one of the girls who worked at the Alhambra.

"Lil, another drink, if you please."
"Sure, honey."

Cade turned his attention back to Jensen. "It's called playing cards intelligently," he explained. "When I have a hand that I think can win, I will play it. When I have a hand that I think won't win, I will fold."

"So, what you're sayin' is you ain't got that pair of tens backed up, huh?" Jensen reached across the table and flipped Cade's down cards over. "What the hell? There's another ten in your hole cards. You're a' holdin' three tens 'n you fold? What are you doin' playin' a man's game, if you ain't got no more guts than to bet on three tens?"

"You were so anxious to bet, I figured maybe you had a full house, or four of a kind," Cade replied.

"Jensen, you cheated," Bligh said. "You ain't allowed to look at another player's cards, even when they fold."

"Let it be," Cade said, reaching for the glass Lil returned to him. "Let him look, I don't mind."

"Ha, you should have played your hand!" Jensen said, as a big smile spread across his face after the hand was played out. "I've got three eights, 'n was lookin' to pair up one of my other cards, but didn't do it. You had me beat, but you lost your nerve."

"Better to be cautious than sorry, I always say," Cade said.

Jensen's three eights won the hand, and he pulled the pot back in.

While the next several hands allowed Cade to maintain the lead he had established, he never drew the hand that would let him surge ahead.

"Cade, they's somethin' I been wantin' to ask you," Coulter said.

"I'm playing cards," Cade said. "At least I'm trying to."

"Seein' as how Willis says you own half the Red House, how come it is that you don't hardly never spend no time there?"

"Mr. Coulter, are you saying you don't enjoy my company?" Cade asked.

"What? No, I ain't a' sayin' nothin' like that. I was just wonderin', is all."

"I suppose it does seem odd," Cade replied without further explanation. "Ace high, I bet ten dollars."

"You're feelin' pretty bold on that ace," Bligh said, sliding ten dollars into the pot.

"Ha!" Jensen said as the next card doubled up his jacks. "Twenty dollars."

Cade, Coulter, and Bligh matched his bet.

The next two face up cards for Jensen were queens, so that he now had two pair showing: queens and jacks. He smiled, broadly, as he examined his hole cards.

Cade had a pair of aces, showing.

"Well now, this is the hand I've been looking for," Jensen said. "Fifty dollars." He pushed the money into the pot. "Boys, that makes the pot better 'n two hunnert dollars."

"That's too rich for me," Coulter said. "I'm figurin' you have a full house, 'n whether it's queens or jacks up, you've got me beat. I fold."

"Me too," Bligh said. "I've already stayed in this game too long." As Coulter had before him, Bligh dropped his cards on the table.

"It's up to you, McCall," Jensen said.

Cade made a big show of studying his hole cards, then looked at his 'up' cards, consisting of a pair of aces, a nine, and a seven. He looked at Jensen's queens and jacks.

"What about it McCall? You goin' to match my bet?" Jensen asked.

"No," Cade said.

"I didn't think so." Jensen reached for the pot.

"Not so fast," Cade said. He smiled. "I'm not going to match your bet; I'm going to see your fifty dollars, then raise it by a hundred. You see, unlike the others, it won't make any difference to me whether you have a full house or not."

"What do you mean you don't care if I have a full house or not? What the hell have you got that you're bettin' so hard? You ain't showin' nothing but a pair of aces'."

Cade smiled. "It'll cost you a hundred dollars more to find out."

Jensen put his hand on his money and started to slide it out, then he stopped and pulled it back.

"No. Hell no," he said. "If you folded on three tens a while ago, there ain't no tellin' what you got there now. You got two aces showin', 'n even if you have another'n in the hole, it wouldn't beat a full house. Only, you said, you don't' care whether I have a full house or not. There ain't no more aces up." Jensen sighed. "Son of a bitch. You got four aces, don't you?"

"Could be," Cade said. "Or, I could have an aces up full house. Either way, I would have you beat."

"There's already over two hunnert dollars in that pot, 'n one hell of a lot of it's mine. I hate givin' it away, but there ain't no sense in throwin' good money after bad. I fold."

Cade reached for the pot.

"Wait, I got to see that hand," Jensen said, and before anyone could stop him, he flipped the cards over. "What? You ain't got nothin' else!" he shouted. "A pair of aces? You bet all that money on a pair of aces? Hell, I had you beat showin'!"

"That you did," Cade replied.

The other two players laughed. "It's called runnin' a bluff, Jensen. He suckered you in good."

"You son of a bitch!" Jensen shouted, standing up so quickly that his chair fell over behind him. He had a gun in his hand.

"I'm about to put your lights out, you damn…"

That was as far as he got before there was an explosion of gunfire. The others, who were shocked to see that Jensen had drawn on Cade, were even more shocked to see that, despite the fact that Jensen had drawn first, it was Cade who fired first.

"How the hell did you…" Jensen started to say, then he fell backwards onto the floor.

Cade, who had the disadvantage of drawing his pistol from a seated position, now held the smoking revolver in his hand.

"I'll be damn," one of the saloon patrons said. "I ain't never seen nothin' like that. Nothin' at all like that."

"I guess this ends our game." Cade stood and raked in the money, then headed for the door.

"Is he dead?" someone asked.

Bligh squatted down beside Jensen's body. His unseeing eyes were open, and the expression of shock was still on his face.

"He's deader 'n a doornail," Bligh replied.

"I didn't think anyone could beat Jensen," another replied.

"Jensen pulled his gun first, 'n he was standin' up. McCall not only beat 'im, he was sittin' down when he done it," Coulter said.

Down at the apothecary, the board of directors had just been voted in. The seven men selected were Robert Wright, Herman Fringer, Henry Stitler, Lyman Shaw, W.S. Tremaine, Edward Moale, and Jeter Willis.

"In testimony whereof we hereunto set our hands and affix our seals the day and year above, written," Charles Rath read, and twelve men signed as witnesses.

Just as the last man signed, someone came running into the building.

"There's been another shooting!" he shouted. "There's been another man killed!"

"Who was it?" Collar asked. "Who was killed?"

"I'm not sure, I heard Dooley Coulter talkin' and he said it was Cade McCall."

"What?" Jeter shouted. "Are you sure it was Cade?"

"I'm ain't sure…but I *am* sure he was one of the ones that was in the shootin'. It happened down at the Alhambra, 'n the other'n that was in the fracas was Cap Jensen. 'N from what we all know about Jensen,

I'd say it's more 'n likely it was McCall who was killed."

"Jeter, I'm sorry," Wright said. "But if it is Cade, you can't really be all that surprised. He's been flirting with the devil ever since his wife died."

"No," Jeter said, shaking his head. "You don't know my friend."

Leaving the meeting, Jeter ran down to the Alhambra.

"No, it warn't McCall that was kilt," Bligh said. "It was him that done the killin'."

"It was Cap Jensen what was the one that was kilt," Coulter said. "He's lyin' back in the storeroom right now, seein' as how Eb Collar ain't down at the mortuary."

"I'll tell you this. Jensen brung it on his ownself," one of the other witnesses reported. "McCall was a sittin' in his chair when Jensen drawed on him."

"Where's Cade now?" Jeter asked.

"Don't rightly know. He picked up the pot and got out of here," Coulter said.

"Thanks," Jeter said, hurrying out of the saloon.

It wasn't hard to find Cade. When Jeter entered the Essington, he saw him in the restaurant sitting alone, eating quietly as if nothing had happened. Cade always had been someone who never got rattled, but to see him eating so calmly after just facing down a known killer seemed rather odd.

Jeter studied his friend for a long moment before going in to speak to him. He wished there was some way he could take the pain from Cade's soul.

Cade glanced up at Jeter when he approached the table, but he didn't stop eating.

"Do you mind if I join you?" Jeter asked.

"Have a seat."

"You had a little excitement, I hear," Jeter said as he pulled out the chair.

"If you call killing a man excitement," Cade answered as he applied pepper sauce to his pork and beans.

"You know you can eat free at the Red House anytime you want."

"No need for me to be cutting into your profit."

"Well, if you feel that way, you could pay," Jeter said with a smile.

"Why should I pay for it, if I can eat free?"

The smile on Jeter's face faded. "Yes, why indeed?" he replied.

"What are you doing here, Jeter? Isn't there some sort of meeting, organizing the town, or something?"

"The meeting's over. I was elected to the board of directors," Jeter added, the smile returning.

"I can't think of a better man for the position."

"Thanks."

"Did you just come to tell me about the meeting?"

"No. I wanted to make sure you're all right."

"If you heard about the shooting, then you probably knew I wasn't killed."

"I wasn't talking about bullet wounds."

"Cap Jensen isn't the first man I've ever killed, Jeter. And I dare say you've killed a few yourself."

"Yes, but…"

"But what?" Cade asked.

"Nothing," Jeter said. He shook his head. "Nothing at all. By the way, when are you coming to see Chantal? You know damn well Magnolia would welcome you to our home at any time."

"I'll get around to it one of these days."

"She's your daughter, Cade. Don't you feel any responsibility at all for her?"

"She is *not* my daughter!" Cade said, slamming his spoon down on the table for emphasis.

"No . . . I . . . don't suppose she is," Jeter replied in a voice that seemed even quieter, and more controlled, by contrast.

"She's my responsibility, because I made a promise to Arabella," Cade said. "But she isn't my daughter."

"Magnolia was there when you made that promise. She told me you promised Arabella that you would never abandon her. Is that true?"

Cade didn't answer.

"Perhaps if you got to know her, you'd come to regard her as your own. I know I couldn't love little Bella more if she was my own flesh and blood." Jeter paused to gauge if Cade was hearing what he was saying. "I don't think about who the real father is, even though I know what Magnolia had to endure to get her here. My situation is the same as yours, you know."

"No, your situation is *not* the same as mine," Cade said through gritted teeth. "Your wife is alive, my wife is dead."

"You are one selfish son of a bitch." Jeter said, as he stood.

"Look, if Chantal is getting to be too much for Magnolia to handle, I'll be glad to hire a woman to look after her," Cade said sharply.

An expression of anger flashed across Jeter's face for a second, then the anger was replaced by hurt.

"That's not it at all. You know damn well Magnolia loves that child like she was her own." Jeter started to leave, then turned back. "We've been friends for a long time, and we've come through a lot together. Is it all to end here, like this?"

Cade just sat there looking down at his plate. Finally, he sighed, almost as if in surrender, lay his spoon down and looked up at Jeter, losing some of the bitterness in his eyes as he did so.

"You're right. You and Magnolia have been nothing but decent people to me and I've done nothing to earn such good heartedness. I tell you what. If Maggie can cook up one of those meals like she used to, I'll be there for supper tonight."

Jeter smiled. "It's a deal."

Chapter Six

THAT NIGHT, Cade McCall stood for a moment in front of Jeter's house, its red shutters and red door reminding him of the Red House in Galveston. He remembered the hurricane that had taken it away, and how Arabella had stayed with him until the end, insisting that she be one of the last to get in the makeshift boat that had kept them safe during that long night.

How could he have been so lucky to have found her, and so unlucky to have lost her? And now he was about to enter this house and see the child whose birth had caused her death.

He couldn't do it. Turning, he hurried down the path hoping to get to the first saloon he could find. And then he heard a familiar voice.

"*Bonjour*, Cade. *Bienvenue chez nous.* Welcome."

Cade stopped. The French. He hadn't heard the soft lilt in a long time, and tears began to well in his eyes.

"No, no, no," he said under his breath, but then he felt Magnolia's presence behind him. Turning around, he saw her, as tears streamed down her face. She opened her arms and pulled him to her in a healing embrace. They stood there for almost a full minute with neither saying a word. It was then that Cade realized this was the first time he had touched any woman since Arabella's death.

He broke the contact and Magnolia took his hand as they walked up the path to the steps.

"*Zheeter* said you would be here for dinner this evening. You've been absent for too long."

"I didn't think you would have wanted to see me," Cade replied.

"That's not true, Cade. Had it not been for you, none of us—not me, not Bella, not Chantal—none of us would be alive. We would have died, too," Magnolia said. Then a smile crossed her face as she opened the door. "Come in. You need to see these beautiful children."

When Cade stepped into the house, he saw two little girls sitting on the carpet. Both had black eyes and black hair. One pulled herself up and began to walk while the other started crawling toward Magnolia. When they reached her, she bent over and picked both of them up.

"Which is which?" Cade asked.

"Few people can tell," Magnolia said as she kissed each of the girls, "but the walker is Chantal. Even though she's the youngest, she does everything first."

"She's going to be a spunky one, just like her mama," Cade said.

Magnolia laughed. "Yes, there was nothing Arabella wouldn't try. Would you like to hold her?"

Cade's eyes opened wide as he stepped back.

"I don't…I don't…"

"You don't know what to do," Jeter said as he moved toward them. "Well, it's easy. You just love them." He took Bella from Magnolia's arms and began to blow on the child's neck, causing her to laugh.

"Here," Magnolia said handing Chantal to Cade. "I need to see how our dinner is coming along."

Cade stood awkwardly holding Chantal, and smiling at him, the little girl rubbed her fingers on Cade's lips.

But it wasn't her fingers Cade felt. He felt a dizziness, and then, just on the other side of his memory, Arabella was there, so beautiful, and looking up at him with eyes that reflected not fear of dying, but her joy at seeing him.

She rubbed her fingers over his lips.

"Cade, promise me you'll take care of her."

"I will," Cade said quietly, embracing the little girl and feeling for the first time a love for her that until this moment, had been suppressed. "I will," he said again.

Jeter was on his hands and knees playing a game with Bella, first putting a cloth over his head and letting her pull it off. Watching them play, Cade was suddenly envious of Jeter. What a fool he had been, denying himself this connection to Arabella.

"Hello, Cade." Chantal immediately held out her hands to the woman who was approaching, and, reluctantly now, she took her from him.

"These girls do love their grandmother," Jeter said.

"It's *Grande-mere*," Mary Hatley said. "It's so good to see you, Cade, even though you do look a little peaked."

Cade laughed. "I'm afraid my life is a little different now than it was when we were in Texas."

"Ha. There's nothing wrong with an honest day's work," Mary said as she took Chantal into the kitchen.

"I take it Mary doesn't approve of square games."

"That's not it," Jeter said getting up. "She cares for you, and she doesn't like to see what you've become."

"A gambler? But yet she accepts you as a saloon keeper?"

Magnolia stepped out of the kitchen. "Are we ready to eat?"

"I'm starved," Jeter said, happy to end the conversation.

"Uhmm, that was delicious," Cade said after dinner as he pushed away what had been a most generous second helping of buffalo stew. "Maggie, if you weren't already married, I'd marry you, just for your cooking."

"It's good to see you teasing," Jeter said. "Is it possible that we're going to see the old Cade again?"

Cade was silent for a long time before he spoke. "I have been a horse's ass for a while, haven't I?"

"No you haven't," Jeter said.

"Really? Can you actually say that?"

"Of course I can. A horse's ass serves a purpose, that's where his hind legs are attached," Jeter said with a little laugh. "Cade, for the last year, you have been…" Jeter paused, looking for a word.

"Un total inadapté," Magnolia interjected. "A total misfit."

"A real bastard," Jeter added, finding the word to complete his own sentence.

Cade pinched the bridge of his nose. "I can't argue with either one of you," he said. "If I had run across someone like me, two years ago, I would have shunned him like a polecat. I'm sorry, it's just that . . ."

"I know you miss her, Cade," Magnolia said. "Arabella was my best friend, and I'm still grieving for her. But you have to get on with your life. This drinking...when I heard about Cap Jensen...that could so easily have been you."

Cade shrugged his shoulders. "Well, it wasn't."

"This time," Jeter said.

"I really should be getting back," Cade said rising from the table. "Thanks for the meal, and I sincerely mean this. Thank you for everything you're doing for Chantal. Arabella would be pleased."

"Don't stay away so long," Magnolia said. "We miss you." She kissed him on the cheek and then busied herself clearing the table.

Cade planned to go back to The Alhambra and catch a game, but as he passed the Red House he decided to step inside. When he did, there was a look of surprise on Pete Cahill's face.

"Hey boys, look what tin pot gambler just rolled in," Pete said.

Cade smiled as he extended his hand. "Is that any way to talk to your boss?"

"Oh...I guess I was out of line. It's just that we ain't seen you in here for a while. Hell, I don't think I've ever seen you in here. What'll you have?"

"Whiskey and a seat at a table," Cade said. "No, I changed my mind. Make that a beer."

Cade made his way back to a table. Jack Reynolds had just sat down and was beginning to deal. "There's room for one more."

Cade recognized the other three players as Johnny Langford, Matt Sullivan, and Isaac Morehouse.

"It's good to have some fresh blood in here," Sullivan said. "Maybe you'll change our luck."

"Oh?" Cade said as he took his seat.

"Reynolds seems to be doing all the winning."

"Well, maybe I can take some of it from him," Cade suggested.

Reynolds looked at Cade. "Maybe you will," he said.

Cade was somewhat confused by the expression on Reynold's face when he made the comment. It was neither challenging, nor acknowledgement of the possibility. The only word he could think of was devious. Was Reynolds cheating? Is that why he was winning so consistently?

The game was five card draw, and Cade drew three sixes on the first hand. Discarding two, he drew another six, and won the hand easily, raking in the fifty-dollar pot.

Two hands later he won with a full house, and the next hand with a flush.

"You changed the luck all right, Cade," Langford said. "The only thing is, you changed it to you."

"Yeah," Morehouse said. "Reynolds, I take it all back, what I was a thinkin'."

"What was that?" Reynolds asked.

"Well, I don't ever want to accuse a man of cheatin', 'less I can see it right out. But I was wonderin' how it was that you was winnin' so much, only now it's McCall that's doin' all the winnin'."

"That's the luck of the game," Reynolds said.

When Reynolds dealt this hand, Cade saw it. Reynolds was good at it, as good as anyone Cade had ever seen, but he had put a palmed card on the deck just before he dealt Cade's hand. Despite the palmed card, Cade had another winning hand.

At first he couldn't understand what was going on. Reynolds was cheating, but he was cheating to Cade's advantage.

Then Cade understood. Reynolds was parking all the money with Cade so that the others wouldn't realize what was happening. Reynolds could start winning now, and take back all the money Cade had won without arousing anyone's suspicion.

Cade was holding an ace high flush. This was a good hand, one that would entice him to stay in the game to the last bet.

"Twenty dollars," Morehouse said.

Langford made the bet.

"I'm out," Cade said, dropping his cards face down. He began to pick up the money that was in front of him.

"You can't leave the game, you son of a bitch!" Reynolds said. "Not with all the money you've won."

"Wait a minute, are you suggesting that we weren't playing for keeps?" Cade asked. "If that's the case, you should have told me before I sat down."

"You ain't leavin' this table!" Reynolds pulled his pistol and pointed it at Cade.

"Hold on here, Reynolds, what do you think you're doin'?" Langford asked.

"I'm goin' to shoot this sonofabitch if he tries to quit this game," Reynolds said, angrily.

Reynolds was so fixated on Cade, that he didn't notice Sullivan get up from his seat, just to his right. Sullivan pulled his pistol, then brought it down sharply on the side of Reynolds head. Reynolds fell forward across the table.

"Well, I guess that shut him up," Langford said.

"Oh, Jesus," Morehouse said. "You killed him, Matt."

"No I didn't," Sullivan answered. "I just hit him in the side of the head."

"Look at his temple."

There was a black hole in Reynold's temple, from which dark red blood was slowly oozing.

Sullivan looked at his pistol. The hammer was blood red, and he saw, at once, what had happened. The spur of the hammer had penetrated Reynold's temple.

"Damn," he said. "I did kill him, but I sure as hell didn't mean to."

"It weren't your fault," Langford said. "You thought you was just a stoppin' a killin'."

The next morning, Cade was lying on the bed when there was a knock on the door.

"Come in, it's open," Cade called not getting up.

"Don't you even bother to lock your door?" Jeter asked as he stepped in.

"Why should I?"

"Oh, I don't know. You've been in town less than a week, and you've been at the scene of two killings."

"I didn't have anything to do with that one last night."

"You were at the table, and Jack Reynolds didn't have an idea in hell who you were—that's why he was setting you up. Pete told me how it happened."

"Then you know it wasn't my fault."

"You might not like what I have to tell you, but I think you should lay low for a while. Get out of town before someone comes gunnin' for you," Jeter said.

Cade took a deep breath. "And I suppose you have a place for me to hide out."

"I do, but it's not what you think. Raymond Ritter's the subcontractor for Wiley & Cutter, and they're the ones who are doing the grading for the railroad. They've got a crew workin' between Fort Dodge and here, and one of their guys just quit."

"Are you saying you want me to work on the railroad?" Cade asked.

"Indirectly, yes. This grading crew only has a few more miles to do," Jeter said. "If you did a little hard labor, it might help you get your head straight. Can I tell Ritter you'll take the job?"

"How much will it pay?"

"Not as much as you made last night, but there won't be anyone pointing a gun at you either."

"How do you know how much I made?"

"Everybody knows. It was close to a thousand dollars."

Cade laughed. "So everybody knows."

Chapter Seven

THE SLATER BROTHERS were camped for the night on Soldier Creek.

"You think there's any Injuns around here?" Weasel asked.

"We ain't in Injun territory," Mack said.

"Neither was the Johanssons, but they was all kilt by Injuns."

"Weasel's right. The Johanssons was kilt 'n they was home at their own farm."

"That was more 'n likely no more'n a couple o' Injuns out just to make some trouble," Mack said. "We ain't as likely to be kilt by Injuns as we are to die from our own stink. I think we should take us a bath here while the creek's up. When we get into town 'n get the money, I aim to find me a whore. 'N when I get me one, I don't want to be stinkin'."

"Good idea," Weasel said.

"Luke, you got another pair o' trousers in your saddle bag?" Mack asked.

"Naw, just a shirt 'n a pair o' socks."

"You need to wrench out them pants you're a wearin'. You ain't washed 'em in a coon's age and they're damn near walkin' by their ownselves."

"I been thinkin' I might want to do that," Luke agreed. He turned the pockets inside out, and when he did a paper floated to the ground.

"What's this?" he asked as he stooped to pick it up.

"How the hell are we supposed to know? It was in your pocket," Weasel said.

Luke frowned as he looked at the paper. "I can't figure this out. Here, you read it."

"I know what it is," Mack said. "Don't you remember when we got into that fight with McCall...back in Caldwell?"

"Sure, I remember. Old Dusty cost us $300," Luke said.

"McCall had raised your bet and put up a saloon he said he owned to cover it. This here's that paper."

"That's when I shot the cards out of his hand," Weasel said. "He had a full house and he would have for sure took the pot."

"But I don't know exactly how I come up with this paper, seein' as how there warn't really no bet placed, on account of it was like Weasel said."

"You must've scooped it up with the money when it got scattered on the floor," Weasel said.

"Well, it ain't worth nothin'." Luke grabbed for the paper.

"Hold on a minute, big brother." Mack read the note.

Redeemable for $ 250.00
Red House Saloon as Collateral
Cade McCall

"This could be worth a whole lot."

"How can it be worth anythin' when the hand wasn't even played?" Luke asked.

"That don't matter none, you've got a signed sheet of paper that says it's redeemable for two hunnert 'n fifty dollars," Mack pointed out.

"Yeah, now that you mentioned it, I do, don't I?"

As Mack continued to study the paper, a broad smile spread across his face. "Boys, this ain't for two hunnert and fifty dollars."

"What do you mean?" Weasel asked. "That's what it says don't it?"

"You see the space between the dollar sign 'n the two?"

"Yeah."

"Looks to me like there'd be enough room to put another number in there," Mack said.

"Yeah," Luke agreed.

"Why you could put a one in there 'n turn it into twelve hunnert 'n fifty dollars real easy," Weasel suggested.

"It'd be just as easy to turn it into seven thousand, two hunnert 'n fifty dollars," Mack said.

"That's why you're the smart one, Mack," Luke said.

"Soon as we get somewhere's so I can get a pen 'n ink, I'll do that very thing."

"Only thing is, I doubt if McCall even has two hunnert 'n fifty dollars, let alone seven thousand, two hunnert 'n fifty dollars," Weasel said.

"No, but he's got a saloon," Mack said.

"What good is that to us? We don't even know where it is."

"Are you kiddin'? All we have to do is ask around. There can't be too many saloons in this part of the country called the Red House," Mack said. Somebody'll tell us where it's at."

"If we was to own a saloon, does that mean we could have all the liquor 'n whores we wanted?" Weasel added.

"Wait a minute," Luke said. "Are you sayin' we could get us a saloon?"

"A saloon, or seven thousand, two hunnert 'n fifty dollars," Mack said. "And the truth is, I don't care which it is."

"Yeah!" Luke said. "It don't matter which it is at all!"

Cade rode out of town the next morning before the sun came up. Raymond Ritter had agreed to hire him for $150, half of what he was paying the other men, which was a pittance compared to what he had picked up at the poker game at the Red House. He felt guilty about taking the money, but it wasn't his fault Reynolds was cheating. Since Dodge City didn't have a bank, he had taken most of the money and put it in the vault that Charles Rath kept at the back of his store. He had held back $300 just in case there was an opportunity to pick up a game with the graders or the track layers.

He hadn't ridden far when he reached the work site.

"Who's the boss?" Cade asked when he slid off his horse.

"Who wants to know?"

"That would be me, Cade McCall."

"Ed Masterson," the man replied with a ready grin. He shook Cade's hand, then took him over to the other two men. "This is Theo Deger, and the young banty rooster there is my brother."

"William Barclay Masterson," the young man said, as he took off his hat and bowed. He was obviously the youngest of the three men, not appearing to be more than eighteen years old.

"That's quite a mouthful," Cade said.

"Don't pay him any mind," Ed said. "Everybody calls him Bat."

"Then Bat it shall be," Cade said.

"Cade McCall? You're the gentleman who dispatched the late Cap Jensen, aren't you?" Bat asked.

"Dispatched?"

"Vanquished, defeated, subdued, subjugated."

"Killed," Theo added.

Cade tilted his head, not quite getting the drift of the conversation.

"You'll have to get used to that," Ed said with a chuckle. "Bat's always learning new words and using them as soon as he learns 'em. He carries a dictionary."

"It is my intention to be a writer someday," Bat said. "And words are the tools of a writer's trade, just as a saw and hammer are the implements employed by a carpenter."

"Or a pair of mules and a draw grader for this job," Theo said.

"I can understand that," Cade said. "And, because you called me a gentleman, may I take it that Jensen wasn't a friend of yours? I would not like to think that you're planning any type of revenge for him."

"Oh, heavens no," Bat replied, resolutely. "You may disabuse yourself of any thought that I have such an idea in mind. I once had the displeasure of playing a few hands of poker with Jensen. I found him to be an uncouth reprobate, a despicable, contumacious cur with less redemptive tissue than an outhouse cockroach, as well as a person of moral turpitude and questionable parentage."

"In other words," Ed added, "Jensen was a low-assed, mealy-mouthed son of a bitch."

Cade laughed out loud. "Why don't you tell me what you really thought of him?"

"Anyhow, it's good to have you with us, in case the Indians decide to pay another visit."

"You've had Indian trouble?"

"Not really. A couple renegades tried to take our stock but Theo scared them off," Ed said. "I wish there would have been more."

"You wanted more Indians? That's a little hard to believe."

"If there were more than just a few, the army would provide us with an escort. As it is, there are so few Indians out making mischief, the colonel doesn't think it's worth it, so that means we're on our own."

"Yes, I can see that."

"Have you ever had to fight Indians before?" Bat asked.

"A time or two," Cade replied without giving any specific details.

Chapter Eight

"THERE HAS TO be a better way of making a living than this," Bat Masterson said, pouring a dipper of water over his head as the hot summer Kansas sun beat down upon him. "I've never worked this hard in my life."

"Quit your whinin'," Ed replied. "Last winter all I heard was how cold your fingers were, how you couldn't hang on to your knife, how you'd never skin another buffalo, how you'd never complain about the heat again."

"I have decided I am a gentleman," Bat said. "I am as out of place performing physical labor, as would be a pig on a dance floor."

"Would that be Fat Tom Sherman's dance floor?" Theo asked, with a chuckle.

"As a matter of fact, considering some of the men I've seen there, I suppose you could say that pigs have already appeared on a dance floor," Bat replied.

After a long day's work, Cade, who was lying on the grass nearby, his hands laced behind his head, laughed.

"What about you, Cade? Have you ever worked this hard?"

"I was raised on a farm in Tennessee," Cade replied.

"That's your answer? You were raised on a farm?"

"If you knew anything about farming, you'd know that was answer enough," Cade replied.

"I figured it must be something like that. You sure don't complain much."

"Actually, I'm glad to have this job."

"Needing money, are you?"

"It isn't the money. Working this hard has been…" Cade searched for some way to explain, "…good for my soul."

"What do you mean?"

"I've sorta been an asshole," Cade said.

"It's takes a big man to admit that. What happened?"

For the next hour, Cade told the story of Arabella, how they had met, holding nothing back, including the fact that she had been a prostitute who arranged for him to be shanghaied, then how they wound up falling in love and marrying . . . and finally the fateful cattle drive where she was kidnapped.

When he first started telling the story, the others laughed at his being shanghaied, but the laughter turned to sorrowful faces when he reached the end of the story.

"I'm glad you found those bastards, and sent them to hell," Bat said.

"I thought, while I was looking for them, that once I'd killed them, I'd be at peace," Cade said. "But it didn't work like that."

Cade smiled, then continued. "But, my friend, Jeter, suggested that I take this job, and he was right. The hard work has given me a chance to think—to stop feeling sorry for myself. Gentlemen, you are looking at a changed man."

The Slater brothers were in Dodge City, occupying a table at George Hoover's saloon.

"I've tried to find McCall to tell 'im that he owed me this money, so I done some checkin' around, 'n found out that he ain't here. He's workin' for the railroad."

"Workin' for the railroad? Why's he workin' for the railroad if he owns a saloon?" Weasel asked.

"Damn, maybe he don't own no saloon," Luke said, disgustedly. "He pulled one over on us, is what he done."

Mack smiled. "Oh, he owns the saloon, all right. Only he owns just half of it, 'n he don't do none of the work there. His partner, a feller by the name of Jeter Willis, is the one that actual runs the saloon."

"How do you know that?" Luke asked.

"I've asked around."

"Yeah? Well that still don't do us no good now, does it?" Luke replied. "I mean, we can't hardly go to this Willis guy 'n show him this piece of paper 'n tell him that he owes us seven thousand, two hunnert 'n fifty dollars. It ain't his name that's on the paper."

"That don't matter none whether his name's on the paper or not," Mack said. "His partner's name's on the paper."

"What good is that?"

"Remember when Lloyd Pugh borrowed that money from pa, 'n he pledged his farm ag'in it," Mack said.

"Yeah, I remember that." Weasel said.

"Uh, huh. Well, have you forgot that Pugh didn't own the whole farm by his ownself. Paul Albertson owned half of it, only the law said when Pugh pledged the farm, that because he was a partner, well he was pledgin' it for Albertson too. That's how it was that pa wound up with it."

"Yeah, well it didn't do him no good, did it? Pa lost the farm no more 'n a year after that," Weasel said.

"That don't matter none," Mack said. "If that was true for the farm..."

"That means it'll be true for the saloon too," Luke said with a triumphant smile.

"What if he don't give it up?" Weasel asked. "What if he fights us over it? I mean a farm is one thing, but this here is a saloon in a town."

"A town without law," Mack said. "Which we can use."

"What are you talkin' about?" Weasel asked. "How is it we're goin' to use the law when there ain't no law in town?"

"What we are going to use, is the fact that there ain't no law," Mack replied with a broad smile. "Let's find out all we can about this man, Willis. We may be able to come up with a way to persuade him to give up the saloon without fightin' us at all."

"I don't know, Mack," Weasel said. "If he's all set on hangin' on to his business, how we goin' to get him to change his mind?"

"Little brother, if we drag him out of there by his balls, why it just stands to reason that his mind will come along."

That night, Cade, Bat, Ed, and Theo were sitting around the fire having just eaten their evening meal.

"Look at the stars," Theo said. "Why, they are so close you can almost reach up and touch 'em."

"I wonder how many there are," Ed asked.

"More than we can see here," Cade replied. "When I was south of the equator I saw an entirely different night sky. No North Star, no Big Dipper, no Orion's Belt."

"When were you south of the equator?" Theo asked.

"When I was on board the *Fremad,* we sailed down to Argentina."

"Weren't you listening, Theo? Cade told us about being shanghaied," Bat said.

"Yes, but he didn't say anything about sailing down to Argentina," Theo replied.

"I envy you, Cade," Bat said. "To have been shanghaied, to be a soldier during time of war, and not only that, to have been a prisoner of war…oh what I wouldn't give for such experiences as you have had."

"Good Lord, Bat, why on earth would you say such a thing?" Cade asked.

"Don't you understand? Experiences for a writer are like canned goods on the shelf to a grocer. They are our stock in trade."

"How can you call yourself a writer, when you haven't written anything yet?" Theo asked.

"Here is what you should know about a writer," Bat replied. "What you see of a writer…his published work, is but one tenth of him. A writer is like an iceberg. The iceberg beneath the water is nine times larger than the iceberg you see. But it is that part under water that forms the iceberg. I am currently building that nine tenths by collecting experiences, and interacting with men of strength and integrity . . . people whose presence will add to my growth as a writer, and a man. People like Cade," he added, throwing a smile toward Cade.

"If I'm the best you can do, you've made a poor choice," Cade said.

There was no false modesty in his self-deprecating remark. He knew that ever since Arabella died, he had been little more than a misanthrope.

"You know, Cade, when you told us your story it wasn't the first time I had heard parts of it. Ed and I were out on the South Fork last winter, and a man named Wyatt Earp told us about you. He heard it from somebody else who told somebody else. You know how buffalo hunters are . . . they like to tell tales when they get together."

"If you already knew the story, why'd you let me tell it?"

"For two reasons," Bat answered. "First of all, I didn't know Earp's story was about you, but the main reason I didn't stop you was I think you *needed* to tell it. I think telling the story, actually articulating it, as opposed to just thinking about it all the time, was part of this healing you were talking about."

"For a kid, I think you're pretty smart," Cade said.

"The story is that you killed those two men from half a mile away . . ."

"It wasn't half a mile, it was about five hundred yards."

"It was half a mile. When the myth is better than the truth, go with the myth," Bat said with a conspiratorial smile. "And lest anyone questions the method by which they were consigned to eternity, I would respond that recreants like that didn't deserve the honor of being faced down."

Cade didn't answer, because no ready response came to him. Instead he stared into the fire, watching the flames lick and curl around the log that was now gleaming red. A gas bubble trapped in the log popped, and it sent up a little shower of sparks.

"Is it true that you gave the kid to Jeter Willis 'n his wife?" Theo asked.

"No, that's not true," Cade replied. "They're looking out after her for me, but I didn't give Chantal to them. I couldn't do that. Chantal is the only thing of Arabella that I have left."

Even as he said the words, he knew that he was speaking the truth. Chantal, whose very presence had been a painful reminder to him of how Arabella had died, was also a living part of her. She was his child, and from this moment on, he intended to let her know, in every way possible, that he was her father.

The Red House Saloon sat on Front Street between a hardware and a dry goods store. The entire front of the saloon was painted red, with the name, in white across the top of the false front. A handsome structure, it was one of the nicer looking buildings in town.

Luke, Mack, and Weasel had moved from the Hoover Saloon down to the Red House in order to give it a thorough inspection.

"Damn," Weasel said as they stood out in the middle of Front Street. "Ain't that somethin'?"

"It's a fine looking saloon, all right," Luke said.

"What do you say we go inside and look around?" Mack suggested.

The inside of the saloon was long, and relatively narrow, though it was wide enough to have a double row of tables in addition to the bar. There were two heating stoves in the place, one toward the front and the second toward the rear. It being late August, neither of the stoves was being employed at the present, but a subtle aroma hung about each of them which suggested the smell of smoke from the previous winter.

There were at least half-a-dozen men standing at the bar. There were three times that many sitting at the tables and at least six of those were in uniform. Most were playing cards.

A piano player was grinding away at the back of the saloon, and a glass bowl sat on top of the piano to collect tips for his effort. Two attractive young women were working the floor.

"You think them women will come with it?" Weasel asked.

"Why not? They work here, don't they?" Luke asked.

"That there 'n is the one I'm goin' to get first," Weasel said, nodding toward one as he subconsciously rubbed himself on the crotch.

The three men stepped up to the bar and the bartender, who had been drying glasses, draped the towel across his shoulder and moved down to the new customers.

"What'll it be, gents?"

"Whiskey," Luke ordered, and the other two matched his request.

"You the owner of this place?" Luke asked.

The bartender chuckled. "I wish," he said. He nodded his head toward the opposite end of the bar.

"That's the owner," he said. "Well, truth to tell, Mr. Willis only owns half of it, but he's the only one ever does any work." The bartender leaned closer so he could speak in quieter voice. "I shouldn't be sayin' this, but the other owner ain't worth a fiddler's damn. He's never in here."

"It looks like you're doing a pretty good business, being as how it's the middle of the afternoon." Mack said.

"Mister, we're always doing a good business," the bartender said proudly, as he poured the three shots of whiskey. "But you hang around until it gets dark. You won't be able to stir this crowd with a stick, they'll be so many in here."

"What about them two pretty girls there?" Weasel asked. "This Willis feller has his way with them, does he?"

The smile left the bartender's lips, and a hostile expression crossed his face.

"It isn't like that," he said. "It isn't like that, at all. In the first place, Mr. Willis is a married man, with a wife 'n two little girls. He's also got his ma livin' with 'im, so he's not the kind that would prowl around. And as far as these two girls are concerned? They don't do anything like that, either. All they serve here are drinks, and pretty smiles."

"Look, Mister, don't get mad or nothin'," Mack said. "My little brother ain't all that bright, 'n he had no call askin' a question like that. I hope you'll excuse him."

"I'm not the one to do the excusin', I'm not the one that was insulted," the bartender said.

"Yes, sir, well, if you put it like that," Mack said. "Willis 'n them two girls wasn't insulted neither, seein' as they didn't hear what my brother said."

The bartender was quiet for a moment, then the stern expression on his face eased, and he laughed.

"That's right, isn't it? There didn't any of them hear you." The smile left his face. "But I wouldn't take it too kindly if you said 'nything like that again."

"My brother's goin' to be as quiet as a mouse," Mack said. "Come Weasel, let's you, me, 'n Luke find us a table and just sort of enjoy watchin' the pretty girls walk by."

Chapter Nine

One of the girls approached the table chosen by the three brothers, and she greeted them with a smile. "If you gentlemen need another drink, just give me a signal and I'll fetch it for you."

"Thank you," Luke said. "What's your name, honey?"

"It's Suzie."

"Well then, tell me, Suzie, how do you like working here?"

"Oh, I like it just fine," Suzie said. "Mr. Willis is easy to work for."

"He lives here, does he? In the saloon?"

"He used to, but now he and his missus built a new house—a nice one over on Walnut. You'd know which one. It's trimmed in red just like the Red House."

"Sounds like he's a fine, upstanding citizen," Luke said.

"Oh, he is. We're just real proud of him. He's on the board of directors, you know."

"We didn't know that. Thanks for the information," Mack said.

Early the next morning, Luke, Mack, and Weasel were sitting in a wagon they had borrowed from an old man in exchange for a bottle of whiskey. Willis's house had not been hard to find, it being the only one in town with a red door, and now they watched. They saw Jeter come out on to the front porch, kiss his wife and two little girls goodbye, then start down the street heading toward his saloon.

"All right, let's go," Weasel said.

"No, not yet," Mack replied, holding out his hand. "Let's wait until we know he's not coming back."

They waited for at least a half hour, then Mack nodded at Weasel who snapped the reins against the back of the team. When they stopped in front of the house, Weasel remained in the wagon, while Mack and Luke went up to the front door.

An older lady answered the knock, and for a moment, Mack thought they might have come to the wrong house.

"Yes?" the older lady asked.

Luke pulled his pistol and pointed at her.

"Don't say a word, don't make a sound," he ordered, shoving her back into the room.

"Who is it, *grand-mère*?" a beautiful young woman asked, coming into the front room.

"We've come callin' on you," Mack said with a leering grin.

Magnolia gasped when she saw that both men were holding guns, and she stepped in front of the girls who were on the floor.

"What is it? What do you want?" Magnolia asked, fighting to keep her voice calm.

"We want you, all of you," Mack added, taking in the others with a wave of his pistol. "We want you to take a ride with us."

"No," Magnolia said defiantly. "We won't go."

"Then have it your way, missy." He put his gun to Mary's head. "Say good-bye to . . . *Grand-mere*, if that's what you call her."

"Stop," Magnolia said as she rushed toward the man. "Take me. Don't hurt this woman."

Mack smiled. "We won't hurt anybody, if you all come with us, but if you don't . . ." he pointed his gun imitating the action of shooting at each of the two girls. "You'll see what we can do."

The Red House Saloon, having just opened its doors, was empty of customers. Neither Cahill, nor the girls had yet arrived, and Jeter was sweeping the floor when two men came in. They weren't regular customers, but Jeter remembered having seen them the night before.

"You're up bright and early this morning," Jeter said, greeting them with a smile. "But that's all right. Let me get rid of my broom." When he stepped behind the bar he turned to them. "Now what can I do for you?"

"How much money do you have?" one of the men asked.

"What?"

"You heard me. How much are you worth?"

The smile left Jeter's lips. "Gentlemen, I really don't think that's any of your business."

"Oh, but it is my business. You see, I was sorta hopin' we could just settle this by takin' the money 'n movin' on."

Jeter reached under the bar and brought up a double-barrel shotgun. "Mister, if you came here to rob me, you chose the wrong place."

"Here now, we ain't here to rob you, so you can just put the gun away. My name's Mack Slater, 'n this here's my brother Luke. We come to do some business."

"Slater? I know that name. Are you from Caldwell?"

"Well ain't that sweet," Mack said turning to his brother. "He knows us."

"I wouldn't say I know you, but I do know that when you got into a fight with Cade McCall, he gave you more than you could bargain for. Is that what this is about?"

"Ain't you the smart one, though?" Mack said. "Cade McCall is the reason we're here."

"If you've come to finish the fight, you'll find it won't be three against one. If I were you, I'd rethink whatever it is you have planned."

"Oh, we ain't here to do no more fightin'," Mack said. "Like I said, we're here to do business. Business with McCall."

"You're not going to find him here," Jeter said.

"Truth to tell, we didn't much figure he would be here, seein' as how we've heard he don't take no real interest in runnin' this saloon."

"If you didn't expect to find him here, why'd you come?"

"We're here to talk to his partner. Now that would be you ain't it?"

Jeter nodded his head, wondering what they were up to.

"Then I reckon we'll just do our business with you," Mack said. "It's Mr. Willis, ain't it?"

"What's this all about?"

"Well sir, it's this way," Mack said. "It turns out McCall lost a lot of money to my brother. A whole lot of money it was, 'n what he done was, he give Luke a marker for what he owed. I guess what happened is, he got to thinkin' maybe he shouldn't a' done that, 'n that's what started the fight. You see, McCall tried to get the marker back but it was too late, because he done give it to Luke, 'cause he lost the hand that the marker was against. So we have come here to collect."

"How are you going to collect, when he isn't here?"

"Oh, we know he ain't here, 'n that's why we've come to you. We figured maybe you can pay us, 'n then maybe get the money back from your partner."

Jeter sighed, then put the shotgun back under the bar. He opened the cash box.

"All right, how much does he owe you?"

"Seventy-two hunnert, 'n fifty dollars," Luke said.

"What?" Jeter gasped, literally shouting the word.

Luke showed the paper to Jeter.

"This here's the paper he give me for the money, 'n as you can see, he signed it. He owes me seventy-two hunnert 'n fifty dollars. That's why I was askin' about the money. Does McCall have that much money?"

Jeter shook his head. "No," he said, quietly.

"Then I reckon we'll just have to take the money from you."

"Are you out of your mind? What makes you think I have that much money?"

"We sat here last night, and we watched you just rakin' it in. Even the bartender said you was rich. So you've got two ways to make it right. Either you give us the money your partner owes or we take over the saloon and call it even," Mack said.

"What do you mean you'll be taking over the saloon? It was Cade McCall who signed that paper. I don't owe you anything."

"The thing is, we got us a lawyer," Mack lied. "'N this here is what he told us. Bein' as the two of you is partners, whatever one of you signs is the same as both of you signin' it. That means that if we can't get the seventy-two hunnert dollars from McCall, we'll be a' gettin' it from you."

"Go ahead and take it to court," Jeter said. "I'm prepared to fight you for it."

"Oh, I think we can settle this betwixt us without goin' to court at all," Mack said with an evil smile.

"There won't be any settlement, not for the kind of money you're asking for," Jeter said.

"How much is the saloon worth to you?" Luke asked.

"I don't know how much it's worth. To be honest with you, I don't think it's worth as much as you have on that marker."

"You wasn't listenin' to the question. What I asked was, how much is it worth to *you*? Is it worth your family?"

"My family?" Jeter asked, a sick feeling coming over him.

"Take a look out the front window."

When Jeter looked out he saw Magnolia, Mary, Bella, and Chantal sitting in a wagon. There was a man with them.

"That's our brother that's with 'em," Mack said. "Weasel is…well, I don't quite know how to describe him, but Weasel is a little touched in the head. He kind of likes to hurt people."

"You can't do that," Jeter yelled, but even as he was protesting he was thinking of Amon Kilgore and Fred Toombs. Those two had kidnapped Magnolia before, and he wouldn't put it past these men to do it again. Before he asked the question, he knew what he would do. "What do you want?"

"Sign your saloon over to us, and we'll let 'em go," Mack said. He showed Jeter a piece of paper.

> *This here paper is to show that I signed over my saloon to Luke, Mack, and Weasel Slater.*

"As you can see, they's a place there for you to sign," Mack said.

"Are you telling me a lawyer drew this up for you?" Jeter asked after he read it.

"No, I done it myself," Mack said, rather proudly. "Now, unlessen you want your family hurt, you'll sign this here paper like I told you to."

"You can't do that, hold my family hostage and force me to sign over my saloon to you. Why the claim wouldn't be legal."

"Why don't you go to the sheriff? Oh, wait, Dodge City don't have a sheriff, does it? You don't have no law at all, except for this." Luke held up his pistol. "And right now, we seem to be in the catbird's seat. Now, what will it be, Mr. Willis?"

"You'll let them go if I sign that quit claim?"

"You've got my word." Mack lifted his hand. "We don't want to hurt them, but we're sort of usin' them for leverage, I think it's called. We needed somethin' to push you into givin' us what your partner lost fair and square in a poker game. If you don't want to honor your debt, well then that little ole wife of yours . . . she's a feisty one. She won't want to see anything happen to that old woman and those two crying brats." Mack squinted his eyes. "But you can damn sure believe, if we give the signal, our brother will kill 'em right here as we sit, and by the time the law gets here from Hays, we'll be long gone. Now what will it be Mr. Willis?"

Jeter looked through the window again, and saw the fear in the faces of his wife and his mother, as they were trying to comfort the children. He had to trust that these men would not do them any harm if he signed the paper.

"Give me a pen."

"Good man," Mack said when the paper was signed. "Now, how about a drink, on the house, to celebrate? Oh, 'n seein' as this here saloon now belongs to us, why, when I say that the drink's on the house, what I'm really sayin' is that it's on us."

"I don't care to have a drink. All I want is my family back."

Chapter Ten

CADE. BAT, ED and Theo were taking a lunch break while the team of mules, still attached to the draw blade, stood to one side of the graded path, munching on grass.

"According to the railroad engineers we're on track to finish the grading within another week," Ed said.

"One more week to go," Bat said.

"Then we'll get three hundred dollars," Theo said. "To tell the truth, I don't think I've ever had that much money at one time."

"What plans have you made for your fortune?" Bat asked.

"I'm goin' to get a new set of clothes, then I'm goin' up to Emporia to the best restaurant in town, 'n order the most expensive thing they have."

"That would be escargot," Bat said.

"All right, then that's what I'm going to order."

"What if you don't like it?"

"How would I not like it? If it's the most expensive thing they have, then it has to be good, don't it?"

"Theo, do you know what escargot is?" Ed asked.

"No."

"It's snails."

"What? You're kidding me! Who would eat snails, unless they was somewhere starvin' to death? 'N why would a restaurant serve it, 'n why would they charge so much for it?"

"It's considered a delicacy by the French," Bat explained.

"Yeah? Well, this ain't France, and as far as I'm concerned, snails is nothin' but bugs. I reckon I'll just get me a steak."

"Hey," Ed said, pointing to a rider who was approaching. "Isn't that your partner from the Red House?"

"Yes," Cade said with a broad smile. "That *is* Jeter."

Cade stood up and walked out to meet the approaching rider.

"Jeter, what brings you out here? If it's to check on my attitude, well I'll have to tell you, you were right. I've done a lot of thinking since I came out here, and I'm a changed man. Hard work will do that for you."

Jeter had offered no greeting, nor did he respond to Cade's remarks. He said nothing at all as he dismounted, then held out a piece of paper toward Cade.

"What's this?" Cade asked.

"You tell me," Jeter replied.

Cade examined the paper.

Redeemable for $7250.00
Red House Saloon as Collateral

Cade McCall

"What is this? Where'd you get this?"

"I got it from the men who now own the Red House Saloon," Jeter said.

"What are you saying? I don't know anything about this."

"Cade, we've been together for many years. Do you think I can't recognize your writing and your signature?"

Cade didn't reply.

"I am bankrupt, you son of a bitch!" Jeter shouted. "You cost me my saloon, and nearly my family."

"Jeter, I…"

That was as far as Cade got before Jeter hit him with a round house right that knocked Cade down.

Cade got up, rubbing his jaw. "Jeter, I'm sorry."

"Sorry? Sorry? You cost me everything and all you can say is you're sorry?" Jeter hit him again, and again, Cade made no effort to block it, though he did manage to keep his feet.

"Fight back!" Jeter said. "Fight back you son of a bitch!"

Jeter continued his pummeling, but at no time did Cade make an effort to defend himself.

After a few more blows, Cade's eye began to swell shut; he was bleeding from his nose and a cut on his lip. There were also bruises on his jaw.

Finally Jeter stopped hitting him, and he stood there breathing heavily from the effort, and with both hands hanging down by his side.

"You son of a bitch," Jeter said again, though these words weren't yelled, or even spoken harshly.

Rather they were spoken softly, and sorrowfully. "What were you thinking? How could you have done that to me, Cade? To us?"

"I'm sorry," Cade said again.

"You're sorry, all right." Jeter turned away from him, then remounted. From his saddle, he looked down at Cade.

"Don't ever come around me again," he said. "And another thing, you've never wanted to claim Chantal as yours; well you're getting your wish. From now on Chantal is my daughter."

Cade watched Jeter ride away, feeling a lump in his throat. His best friend hated him, but not as much as he hated himself.

"Cade, are you all right?" Bat asked, solicitously. He, Ed, and Theo had stood by, watching the entire confrontation in absolute silence, until this moment.

"Lunch time is over," Cade said. "We've got some grading to do."

When Luke Slater walked into the Pig Lot Saloon in Caldwell, he was greeted by Dusty Coleman.

"I haven't seen you for a while, Slater," the saloon owner said. "And to be honest, I was hopin' I wouldn't be seein' you anytime soon. The last time you were here, you started a fight."

"Yeah, well, you was paid for whatever damage me 'n my brothers done. Is Lola Fontaine here?"

"She's upstairs, but I can get one of the other girls for you."

"No. I just want to see Lola."

"Then you'll have to wait your turn. What'll you have to drink?"

"I don't want nothin'."

"This isn't a waiting room for the stage, Slater. If you're going to sit around in here, you're either goin' to buy a drink or you're goin' to pay rent. Which will it be?"

"I'll have a beer."

Coleman drew a beer and handed it to Slater who took it over to a table that afforded him not only a view of the stairs, but of the first door up on the second landing. He knew that door very well; it was Lola Fontaine's door.

He was half finished with his beer when the door opened and a man came out. He had a smug and satisfied expression on his face, and was still packing his shirt tail in as he started down the stairs. Lola stepped into the door.

"Bye now, Mr. Dimke, you come back, you hear. You're welcome anytime," she called toward the man who was coming down the stairs. Dimke didn't turn back toward her, but he replied to her call lifting his hand and throwing a wave over his shoulder.

Lola closed the door to her room then started down the stairs. She was half-way down when she saw Luke.

"Luke Slater!" she called down to him. "I haven't seen you in a while."

"I've been busy," Luke said.

Lola hurried down to see him, and accepting a coin from him, went to the bar to get a drink for herself before she came to join him at the table.

"So, you came to see me, did you?" she asked with a flirtatious smile. "I thought you and your brothers had left town, but you couldn't stay away, huh? Well, finish your drink and we can go upstairs. I've got a little time available."

"I want to go upstairs with you," Luke said. "But it won't be to dip my dobber."

"Oh? Well, you know that if we go upstairs together, you'll pay for my time whether we do anything or not."

"I know, but I've got something to tell you, and I don't want anybody to hear what I have to say."

"All right," Lola said setting her drink on the table. "Let's go up now."

"Lola, me 'n my two brothers has come into a saloon, 'n it's a damn fine one, too," Luke said once they were in Lola's room.

"A saloon? How'd you come up with a saloon?"

"Let's just say we won it in a poker game. It's over in Buffalo City, only now the folks is callin' it Dodge City, on account of the town's so close to Fort Dodge."

"I know where that is. It's over in Ford County, right?"

"Yeah, that's it," Luke said. "But right now, we've got a problem. This place we got . . . well it's not like the Pig Lot."

"What do you mean? If it's a saloon, it serves liquor doesn't it?"

"It does, but it's got a place where you can get a bite to eat, too."

"And what's wrong with that?" Lola asked.

"Well, Mack thinks we could make more money if we put in a wheel and a faro table, and then built some rooms behind it," Luke said. "And, Lola, that's where you come in. We want you to come over there 'n work for us."

"Good heavens, Luke, you don't think I can handle all your customers by myself do you? I'd be on my back twenty-four hours a day."

"No, no, that's what's good about it. We want you to go to Wichita 'n get some more girls, as many as you can find. They's already another place in town that's got a lot of whores, 'n that's Fat Tom Sherman's dance hall. That's where the buffalo hunters 'n the soldiers go when they want 'em a woman. But I want 'em to start comin' to the Red House."

"The Red House?"

"That's the name of the saloon."

"No," Lola said when she saw the Red House for the first time. She shook her head. "I can't work in the Red House."

"What? If you don't, how are we goin' to get any whores to come in here? You said you'd work for us."

"You're going to have to change the name, and the way this place looks."

"All right, what about Slater's Saloon?" Luke asked.

"Why not call it Jones' Store?"

"What?" Luke replied, confused by the response. "That don't make no sense."

"Neither does calling it Slater's Saloon. You'll need a name that as soon as people hear it, they'll know right away what to expect. And you're going to have to change the way it looks."

"Why? I think it looks fine, the way it's all painted up red 'n all."

"Let me think about it for a while," Lola said. "I'll come up with something."

"That's why I went all the way to Caldwell to get you," Luke said.

"And one more thing. I intend to be in charge of all the girls," Lola said. "I don't intend to work the customers anymore."

"All right," Luke said. "No, wait I'll have to get Mack to go along with that, but I'm sure he'll do it."

"Why do you have to get Mack's permission? You're the oldest, aren't you?" Lola asked.

"It's because everybody knows Mack's the smartest."

Lola laughed. "All right, get his permission."

The next morning, Lola took the stage to Wichita to solicit some girls to work for her. She was pleased that Mack Slater had agreed to allow her to manage the women, even though the lion's share of the money they would earn would go into the coffers of the saloon. She was also pleased that she would not be working on the line. It had been ten years since she left Missouri, where she had seen her ma and pa killed by raiders. She didn't know what had happened to her four brothers, but she assumed they had been killed in the war.

She would always be thankful to Brewster Arnett, for taking her to Kansas City, but when a horse kicked the old man in the head, and knocked him senseless, she was left to make her own way in the world. Mr. Arnett had been kind to her, and she had no idea what a man would do to a woman. But she soon learned, and when she found out men would pay her to lay with them, she made the decision to become a "lady of the evening".

What unkind words those were. She was not a "lady" and she never would be. She was a whore, and nothing more.

When she got to Wichita she watched as the women came and went from the saloons and brothels. Those that were dressed in the finest clothing she didn't approach, but when she saw someone who was dressed shabbily, she knew she had a potential hire.

Many worked from cribs—one room shacks that barely had room for a bed. The girls who worked out of these had to solicit their business, and they often sat in chairs in front of a window actively peddling their bodies. Lola had a certain empathy for these women. It was in just such a situation that she had started out.

Lola walked down the alley where the cribs were located. She felt like she was in a grocery store picking out the best apples in the bin. Some women were unkempt, with overly made up faces. Those she passed on. At last she felt she had her selection. Mack had said he wanted ten girls, but she only chose six.

When she approached one crib, the door swung open.

"Who are you and what do you want?" a young woman asked. "If you're from the law, I paid my fine, and if you're from the Temperance League, just go away."

"I'm neither of those," Lola said. "I've come up from Dodge City to recruit girls to come work for me. I can promise you better money and a clean environment. Would you like to come?"

The woman smiled, and then she opened her door a little wider.

"Yes, I would, ma'am, but there's only one thing. You see that baby lying on the bed. She comes with me."

"A baby. I don't know about that," Lola said.

"Well, she's not really a baby, but she's my baby sister. That's her. She's fifteen years old."

"Does she work on the line?"

"Absolutely not. I would never let Cetti do that."

"Then why is she here?"

"Our ma died back a month or so, and we ain't found a place for Cetti to work yet, so she lives with me. When I'm busy, she spends her time in the woodshed out back."

"That's no place for a fifteen-year-old girl. If some john saw her, why . . . who knows what would happen to her."

"Then can she come with me?"

"Yes, by the way, what's your name?"

"I go by Frankie. Frankie Jones, but my real name's Fannie Marcelli."

"All right, Frankie it is, and I'm Lola Fontaine. Do you think you and Cetti can be ready to go tomorrow morning?"

"I can, but there's one thing, Miss Fontaine. If I go, you have to promise me you won't let Cetti . . . you know."

"I think we can find something for her to do," Lola said.

"Thank you, thank you," Frankie said as she embraced Lola. "We'll be ready as early as you want us to be."

"All right, you two be down in front of the livery tomorrow morning at nine o'clock. I hired a couple of buckboards to take us to Dodge City."

It took them three days to make the trip from Wichita, and during that time the women who had been competitors used the time to become friends. Cetti became a particular favorite of all the others, and they swore they would do whatever they could to keep her off the line.

Chapter Eleven

THE TRACK LAYING was only a week or two behind the grading team, and was due to reach Dodge City in September. Cade, Bat, Ed, and Theo having completed their task, were now back in Dodge City. Here, they were greeted by a smiling Raymond Ritter.

"Outstanding job men, the superintendent told me the last five miles have been some of the best they've had to work with. They finished the last five miles in record time."

"That's good," Cade said.

"Now, what about our money?" Bat asked.

"Oh, yes, your money. Here you go, gentlemen." Bat rubbed his hands together in eager anticipation. Ritter gave each of them a single, twenty-dollar bill.

"Here, what the hell is this?" Theo asked. "I thought we were supposed to get three hundred dollars."

"You are, you are. But you don't expect me to have that much money on my person, do you? This twenty dollars is just to hold you over 'til I can get to Atchison and get your pay from the boss."

"How soon will that be?" Ed asked. "Twenty dollars won't even get us into a high stakes card game, let alone have money left over buy us a new pair of pants."

"I promise you, it won't be long."

"Ritter, we broke our backs out there grading, digging, and sweating," Bat Masterson said. "Speaking for myself, I'm going to be very upset if you don't come through with this money. I'm going to give you two weeks, and if you don't get back, well then, I'm going to hunt you down."

"I told you, you'll get your money," Ritter insisted. He climbed into a buggy and drove away.

"Come on," Ed said, "Let's go get a beer."

"Hey, will you look at that," Bat said.

He pointed to what had been the Red House Saloon. It was now renamed the Devil's Den. It was still painted red, but the false front now sported a paint job of yellow flames, leaping up from the red.

From inside they heard a woman's scream, though it was followed immediately by laughter.

"Come on, let's check it out," Ed suggested.

"No, wait," Bat said. He looked at Cade with an expression of concern on his face. "How do you feel about it, Cade?"

"How do you expect me to feel? Is asshole strong enough?"

"What I meant is do you want to come with us?"

Cade had initially intended to pass the saloon by, but he was interested to see what was going on.

"I guess it won't hurt to have a beer," he said.

A dense cloud of tobacco smoke hovered just under the ceiling. The saloon was crowded with loud and boisterous men, and at least half-a-dozen very scantily clad women moved through the crowd. There were three bartenders, and they were being kept busy.

Cade had to admit that he had never before seen the Red House doing this much business. But then, he reminded himself, this was no longer the Red House. This was the Devil's Den.

Cade and the other three stepped up to the bar. "What'll it be, gents?" the bartender asked.

"Where's Pete?" Cade asked.

"Pete?"

"Pete Cahill. The regular bartender."

"Oh, him. Well, he ain't regular no more. When Mr. Slater took over the saloon all the ones that was workin' here for Willis quit. Now, what'll it be? I ain't got time to stand here jaw-bonin' like this."

All four ordered beer, and even before the mugs were set before them, they heard loud, angry words coming from the floor.

"You son of a bitch!" The angry shout was followed by the sound of shots, and gunsmoke curled in with the tobacco smoke, adding its own acrid scent to the prevailing aroma.

"You kilt 'im," another voice said.

"Damn right, I kilt the cheatin' son of a bitch. Look up his sleeve. I seen 'im put a ace up there."

"There ain't nothin' up his sleeve, Dekus," one of the card players said. "He warn't cheatin' you."

"Well, I thought I seen 'im put a ace up his sleeve."

"That's a hell of a note, to kill someone just 'cause you thought he was cheatin'."

"Yeah? Well, it's been done, 'n there ain' nothin' we can do about it now, is there?" the shooter said. He looked around the saloon. Is there anyone in here who wants to make somethin' out of this here shootin'? 'Cause if there is, do it now."

The shooter was holding his pistol in his hand, a small wisp of smoke still curling up from the barrel.

"Ain't nobody got nothin' to say about it," another said. "You done what you thought you had to do."

"Then somebody drag his body out front so's Collar can take care of it," someone else said. "Dead bodies in a saloon ain't good for business."

Cade recognized the voice of the last speaker, and looking toward it, he saw Luke Slater. He thought about challenging him for taking the saloon, but he was pretty sure that, under the circumstances, his challenge would not reverse Jeter's misfortune. Also, at this point, any challenge as to the valid ownership of the saloon would more than likely end up with one of them being killed.

As he thought more about it, though, the prospect of one or both of them getting killed had little meaning for him. He would just as soon kill Slater as not. And he didn't care what happened to him.

A few minutes later Dooley Coulter stepped up to the bar beside Cade.

"Hello, Cade," Coulter said.

"Dooley," Cade replied tipping his hat.

"Ain't seen you around in a while."

"I've been working," Cade replied.

"I reckon you heard what happened to Jeter," Coulter said. "Hell, you can see what happened, 'cause all you got to do is take a look around this place."

"It's not the bar Jeter ran. I can't see him giving it up without a fight."

"They say Jeter didn' have no choice but to go along with it," Coulter replied. "From what I hear, the Slaters had his family 'n was goin' to commence a' killin' 'em if Jeter didn't sign over the saloon to 'em. 'N so that's what he done. I reckon that just anyone of us would've done the same thing."

Cade didn't reply. If Magnolia and the girls were threatened, Jeter would have had no choice. He couldn't have waited for a court of law to decide the proper ownership of the Red House.

"Cade, did you really bet the saloon on a card game?" Coulter asked.

"I don't know," Cade said. "I . . . I must have. Jeter has the IOU. I've seen it, and it has my writing. But . . .

"Was you drunk?"

Cade was quiet for a moment. "Yeah," he admitted. "I was drunk."

"Well, then, you most likely done it."

"Yes." There was a world of self-condemnation in Cade's single-word, clipped response.

"It's too bad to see a good man like Jeter down and out," Coulter said.

"What's he doing for a living, now?" Cade asked.

Coulter shook his head. "Nothin' much. Sometimes he picks up a dollar or so doin' odd jobs, but he ain't found nothin' regular."

If Cade had not felt the guilt of his actions before he certainly felt it now. Coulter patted him on the shoulder and walked away and no one approached him at the bar.

Cade looked around for Bat and the others, and saw that they were at the back of the saloon playing the Wheel of Fortune which, like the girls, was a new addition to the saloon.

Cade took his beer to a small table that was out of the way and sat down. He decided right then, that he would somehow, some way, make it up to Jeter. It may not be by getting this saloon back, but he would not let Jeter be reduced to a rag picker.

"Would you like some company, Mr. McCall?"

The woman who asked the question was quite pretty, but there was something slightly different about her and it took him a moment to realize what it was. Though she was dressed attractively, her clothes and face paint were not openly provocative as was the other women in the Devil's Den.

"I don't think anyone else will be joining me," he said, as he kicked the chair back with his foot.

"I'm Lola Fontaine."

Cade nodded his head in her directions as he took a drink. "I don't think I've had the pleasure."

"No, we've met before," Lola said.

Cade laughed. "You could tell me anything and I wouldn't remember it. I seemed to have done a lot of stuff that I don't remember."

"I was working in Caldwell at the Pig Lot Saloon and you were…" Lola said.

"Drinking and fighting and spending some time in jail." Cade finished her sentence. "What brought you here?"

"Mack Slater. He hired me to manage the young ladies. If you see any of them that you think you would be interested in, let me know and I'll make the arrangements for you."

"What if I wanted you?"

Lola smiled. "You wouldn't get me. I don't do that anymore."

"Then what would it cost me if I just want you to sit here and keep me company?"

"Buy me a drink," Lola said.

Cade withdrew a coin and handed it to her. "Bring me another one, too."

Cade was half-way through his second beer when Luke Slater came over to the table.

"You can't be wastin' all your time on one customer," he said to Lola. "Especially not this one."

"I'm sorry, Mr. McCall," Lola said with a pleasant smile as she stood. "When you come back, perhaps we can visit again."

Cade nodded.

Slater stood by the table for a moment longer. "You can come in here anytime you want, McCall, just as long as you don't make no trouble. This is my joint and me 'n my brothers is runnin' a peaceful saloon."

"I'd say that," Cade said. "When that man just shot a card player a few minutes ago, that was being peaceful."

"This ain't the only saloon things like that happen in," Slater said, dismissively. He walked away just as Bat and the others returned.

"Did we interrupt something?" Bat asked.

"No," Cade replied. "The son of a bitch didn't want me talking to one of his girls. How'd you do at the new wheel of fortune?"

"Wheel of fortune? Ha. That's a misnomer if there ever was one. They should call it the wheel of insolvency," Bat said.

Cade laughed. "I guess that answers my question."

"What do you say we get out of this den of iniquity, and go down to the Essington and have something to eat?" Bat invited.

"You folks go on," Cade said. "I have something else to do."

"Cade, you aren't going to pick another fight with Luke Slater, are you because if you do, we want to be in on it, too," Bat said.

"No, this has nothing to do with Slater."

Cade made his way to the Rath and Company store. The day before he went out to the grading job, he had put the winnings from the poker game in the vault Charley Rath kept. Alonzo Webster was sitting at a sewing machine where he was making bags for the sugar-cured buffalo humps. He looked up as Cade came into the store, but he didn't stop until he was finished with the bag.

"After what you did to Jeter Willis, I wouldn't think you'd have the nerve to ever show your face in this town again."

Cade let out a long breath. He knew he was going to be treated as a pariah everywhere he went in Dodge City.

"Is Mr. Deckert in the back room?" Cade asked.

"He was. Go on back," Webster said indicating the back of the store with a nod of his head.

Hodge Deckert was a small man who wore his pants so high that his belt line was nearly under his armpits. His thinning gray hair was combed straight back, and he had a small, perfectly trimmed moustache.

"Yes, Mr. McCall?" he said, the greeting more professional than friendly.

"How much money do I have on deposit?" Cade asked.

Deckert picked up a ledger book, and began running his finger down across a column of names.

"It would appear that you have six hundred and thirty-seven dollars and fifty-two cents."

"Give me one hundred and thirty-seven dollars and fifty-two cents," Cade said, writing out a draft.

"Very good sir. That will leave you a nice, round figure of . . ."

"That will leave me nothing. I want you to transfer the rest of the money to the account of Jeter Willis."

"I can do that," Decker said. "I'm sure he will be most appreciative. I hated to turn him down when he asked me for a loan, but with no visible means of support, I just couldn't do it."

"Mr. Willis is not to know where this money came from. Do you understand?"

"No, I don't understand. When he learns that he has money in his account, he'll wonder where it came from."

"You make up a story. Tell him you were going over the books and you found a mistake in the bookkeeping, a mistake in his favor."

"I can't do that," Deckert said. "I've never made a mistake. People wouldn't trust me with their money if I wasn't careful."

"This time you made a mistake. Do you understand?" Cade put his hand on his gun.

"Yes, sir, I believe I made a mistake. I can see it right here."

Chapter Twelve

JETER WILLIS was on the floor playing with the girls when Magnolia came in with a few supplies. A big smile was on her face.

"You'll never guess what happened," she said. "I ran into Mr. Deckert and he told me he had made a mistake. We have five hundred dollars we didn't know we had."

"Are you sure he told you that? That old man never makes a mistake."

"That's what he said, and when I went by Rath and Company, I got twenty dollars."

"That can't be." Jeter withdrew a small account book from one of the pigeon holes in the desk. "Hodge may have made a mistake, but I didn't. Somebody had to deposit money in my name."

"You have so many friends. Which one do you think would do this?" Magnolia asked.

"I don't know, but George Cox told me Cade's back in town. He took another room at the Essington."

"Oh, Jeter, if he did this, we must thank him."

"Never. And if I run in to him, I'll see to it that he takes his damn money back. I'll not let him ease his conscience so easily."

Their conversation was interrupted by a knock on the door.

"You answer it," Jeter said. "If it is Cade, tell him . . . no, never mind. I'll answer the door. I'll tell the son of a bitch myself."

Jeter jerked the door open. "What do you . . ." he paused in mid-sentence when he saw that it was Pete Cahill. "Oh, sorry, Pete, I thought it might be someone else."

"I'm sorry to be bargin' in on you and the family but I got me a proposition. I reckon you know I don't work at the Red House anymore," Cahill said.

"I had heard that."

"I just couldn't work for those people, 'N Suzie 'n Nell, why, they couldn't work there neither. I s'pose you've seen what they done with the place, paintin' it like it's on fire 'n callin' it the Devil's Den 'n all. That place is a real hell hole now, with nothin' but the scum of the earth comin' there as customers."

"Yes, but what can I do for you? What do you need?"

"It's not for me, it's for my boss. He told me to find out if you would you like a job."

"A job?"

"Yes, sir. I'm tendin' bar down at the Essington, but now they're calling it the Dodge House. I mean, Mr. Boyd figured that seeing . . . well, since you don't have the saloon no more, he thought you might like a job somewhere else."

"What sort of job?"

"Well sir, Harley Jim, the feller that was tendin' bar with me? He quit, 'n went to work for the Slaters. 'N Mr. Boyd, him and Mr. Cox, down at the Dodge House, he asked me if I thought you'd like to work for 'em. I know it might shame you to work as a bartender seein' as how you actual owned a bar 'n all. But..."

"Nonsense, Pete, no honest work is shameful. I'll be glad to talk to Mr. Boyd and Mr. Cox about the job," Jeter said. "And thank you, for coming."

Pete smiled. "Gee, Mr. Willis. It'll be great, workin' with you again."

"Yes, but, under the circumstances, I think calling me Jeter, instead of Mr. Willis, would be more appropriate."

"Yes sir, uh, Mr. Jeter," Pete said.

Two days after Jeter started working as bartender for the Dodge House Saloon and Restaurant, George Cox, asked Jeter to step into his office to speak with him.

"Is there a problem with anything, George?" Jeter asked. "Excuse me, I mean Mr. Cox."

"You've called me George from the first time we met, Jeter. Just because you've come here under some difficult circumstances doesn't mean we aren't still friends."

"I appreciate that," Jeter replied.

"I have something I want to suggest. Actually, it involves your wife."

"Magnolia? Uh, George, I don't think . . ." Jeter shook his head. "I don't think she'd want to work here, and with Suzie and Nell joining the help you already had, you don't really need another girl."

"No, no, you misunderstand," Cox said, holding up his hand. "I don't want her working in the bar; I want her to be my cook."

A broad smile spread across Jeter's face. "She's the best cook I've ever known. When would you want her to start?"

"Tomorrow would be good," Cox said.

The very first train to roll into Dodge after the railroad was completed took place on a fall day in September. The engine had been polished for this special run and the boiler gleamed black in the sun. The cab was red, with gold lettering: *AT&SF 2752*, while the brass trim glistened. It had a high, fluted stack from which smoke was drifting, the steam relief valve was opening and closing to vent off steam, and the engineer who had brought the train in was leaning through the window of the red cab, smiling down at the gathered crowd. A photographer had set up his camera and was now bent over beneath the cape to get his photo.

The first train to reach Dodge had brought no passengers, nor was it configured to take any passengers back with it. Instead it was a freight train, and would be taking buffalo hides back East when it departed.

The train had also brought a box car which it parked on a side track. Until such time as a depot could actually be built, the box car would serve that purpose.

This was the most exciting thing that had ever happened in Dodge, and there were two or three hundred people who had come to witness the historic event. They were in high spirits, because the railroad not only guaranteed the survival of the city, but its growth as well. As the unofficial spokesman of the town, Robert Wright used the opportunity to make a speech.

"Ladies and gentlemen, take a look at what stands before you on this day. You think you see sitting there, an engine of the Atchison, Topeka, and Santa Fe Railroad, complete with all the inner workings and hidden mechanisms that provide locomotion; the steam cylinders, the piston rods, and the drive wheels. Ah, but that, my friends, is only the surface, the appurtenances by which the locomotive is energized.

"My friends, if your observation goes no deeper than that, then woe betide you, for you are missing a glorious opportunity to see into the future. Yes, ladies and gentlemen of this new and growing city, this is the beginning of a city that will henceforth be known as the Queen of the Plains!"

Robert Wright's short speech was cheered enthusiastically by those who had gathered for the event, citizens of the town, as well as buffalo hunters and soldiers who, while not residents, depended upon the town's existence.

As Cade moved through the crowd he saw Jeter and Magnolia, each holding one of the girls. Like so many others, they had come down to watch the arrival of the first train. He looked at them, paying particular attention to Chantal. He had been wrong, oh so wrong, to have neglected her for so long. While he was working on the railroad, the hard labor had, as Jeter suggested, brought him to the realization that Chantal was a blessing, a living connection to Arabella. He had squandered that opportunity, and now through his own foolishness, he would never have that opportunity again.

"Have you seen Ritter?" Bat Masterson asked, his question bringing Cade back from his musing. "I thought he told us he'd be on the first train into town with our money."

"Well, there weren't any passengers on this train," Theo said. "I expect he'll be on the first train with passengers."

"You have more faith than I do," Ed said. "You know what I'm beginning to think? I think the son of a bitch has run out on us. I don't think he plans to pay us. Hell, I don't think he ever planned to pay us. I believe he was figuring on just keeping all the money the railroad paid him."

"We'll get paid," Bat said.

"What makes you so sure?" Theo asked.

"Because I intend to make certain that we get paid," Bat said.

Chapter Thirteen

THOUGH CADE still kept a room in the Dodge House, as it was now being called, he no longer frequented the saloon. It was, he believed, the best saloon in town, but Jeter was tending bar there, and Cade thought it would be better for both of them if he steered clear of the place.

The beneficiary of Cade's business now was Hoodoo Brown's place, which was one block farther down on Front Street.

Cade and Bat were playing cards in the same game. Bat was a very good player, better even than Cade, but Cade was still winning enough to stay ahead in the game. The other two players in the game changed frequently, as they quickly learned that playing against two players as skilled as Cade and Bat was non-productive for them.

They had just finished a hand, and one of the new players was getting ready to deal when Theo and Ed stepped up to the table.

"He's here," Theo said.

"Who's here?"

"Ritter. He just came in on the train. And, I heard that he has two thousand dollars with him."

"Well," Bat said with a broad smile. "Perhaps we have misjudged the man. Gentlemen, shall we cross the street to the depot and collect our money?"

"What about the game?" one of the other two players asked.

"You can fill our two seats," Cade said. "And you'll probably have a better chance of getting back some of the money that you've lost."

"You've got that right," the other player said.

Happily, Cade, Bat, Ed, and Theo crossed the street to stand on the newly constructed wooden platform.

As they had for every train since the railroad had reached Dodge, many of the citizens of the town had turned out for the excitement of the arrival. This was, effectively, end of track for the railroad, because though construction had continued toward the Colorado state line, this was the last settlement on the track that had thus far been laid.

The four men watched the passengers disembark, but Ritter was not among them.

"Are you sure he's on this train?" Bat asked.

"That's what Max Robbins told me," Theo said "And he works for the railroad, so he should know, and Max's the one who told me he was bringin' money."

"Well, if the son of a bitch is on this train, why didn't he get off?

"You know what I think?" Ed asked. "I think he may have seen us through the window, and decided he didn't want to get off. You did threaten him the last time we saw him."

"You may be right," Bat said. "So why don't I just go aboard to meet the gentleman, and invite him to join us? And while I'm at it, I'll remind him that he owes us one thousand, fifty dollars."

"Nine hundred seventy," Ed said. "Remember, he already paid us twenty dollars apiece."

"Oh yes, to be sure," Bat said, smiling. "Nine hundred seventy dollars."

The train was pulling three bright yellow passenger cars, and Bat climbed onto the first one, then he walked down the aisle looking for his man. Ritter wasn't in that car, nor was he in the second. But Bat saw him as soon as he stepped into the third car. Ritter was sitting with his back to the front of the car, and he was looking out the window, studying the crowd that had gathered to meet the train. As a result of his position and diverted attention, his first awareness of Bat Masterson's presence was when he felt the business end of a pistol being placed behind his ear.

"Mr. Ritter," Bat said in a deceptively pleasant voice. "Welcome to Dodge City."

"What? Is that a gun placed to my head?" Ritter asked in alarm.

"As a matter of fact, it is," Bat answered in the same pleasant voice. "I wonder if you would be so kind as to step off the train with me? Some of your friends are here, and they'd like to say hello."

"This is against the law, you know. You have no right to force me off this train."

"Oh? Well, perhaps you'd like to report me to the sheriff."

"There's no sheriff in Dodge City," Ritter said. "There's no law here at all."

"Oh, but that's where you're wrong," Bat said. "There is law in Dodge City. You might call it the law of the six gun. And that means, that at the moment, I am the law."

"You . . . you wouldn't shoot me."

"Do you really want to put that to the test, Mr. Ritter?"

"N . . . no. I'll leave the train."

"Well, that's very decent of you."

Reluctantly, Ritter stood, then Bat directed him down the aisle to the back door of the car. When they stepped down from the train there were several who noticed that Bat was holding a pistol leveled toward Ritter's head.

"Ladies and gentleman, I apologize for what might seem to you a most discourteous act, I mean, holding a gun on a visitor to our fair town," Bat said. "And I suppose it does show a certain degree of indecorous behavior. But you see I, my brother, Mr. Deger, and Mr. McCall, worked in the heat of the summer, grading the right of way which allowed the tracks to be laid into Dodge. The tracks that brought this very train to town, in fact. And for this backbreaking labor, we were each promised three hundred dollars apiece by this . . . gentleman." Bat set the word 'gentlemen' apart from the rest of the sentence, and applied a sarcastic tone to its pronunciation.

"But, for this work, he gave us each twenty dollars."

"What? Someone in the crowd called out. "Is that true, Mister. Did you cheat these men out of their fair wages?"

"I'm going to pay them," Ritter replied, anxiously.

"Good, good. You have two thousand dollars on you now, I understand. I'm glad that you have come to pay us."

"How did you know I have two thousand dollars?"

"It doesn't matter how I know, does it? I mean, as long as you are here to pay us."

"No, you don't understand. This money is to be used for something else. But you needn't worry, I'll pay you."

"Mr. Ritter, you demanded that we finish the grading within a month's time, and we did that. Now, just as we were timely in carrying out our task for you, so too, should you be timely in paying us."

"But I can't, not with this money."

"Oh, I think you can," Bat said. As he spoke, he pulled the hammer back on the pistol and it made a deadly click as it rotated the next cylinder chamber under the firing pin.

"No, no! Don't shoot me!" Ritter cried out. Reaching down to his belt, he opened the wallet and pulled out a wad of money. "Here! Here is the two thousand dollars!"

"Oh, heavens, Mr. Ritter, please don't misunderstand me. I wouldn't want to give my fellow citizens here the mistaken idea that I am a highwayman. Perhaps If I were robbing you, I would take the entire two thousand dollars. But I'm not robbing you; I am merely collecting a just debt. Now, three hundred dollars apiece for my brother, Mr. Deger and myself, and a hundred fifty for Mr. McCall would be one thousand fifty dollars. However, as you were so . . . generous . . ." again, Bat gave sarcastic emphasis to a word, "as to pay us twenty dollars apiece, we will take only nine hundred and seventy dollars."

Bat handed the money to Ed, who counted out the proper amount, then gave the rest of the money back to Ritter.

"There you are, Mr. Ritter. We are satisfied now that we have been paid in full, and you still have over a thousand dollars with which to carry out your affairs. Now, don't you feel better that your honest debt has been satisfied?"

"You are insane," Ritter said, angrily, as he took the money Ed handed him. He was able to give vent to his feelings because he was now satisfied that Bat wasn't really going to kill him.

"There may well be those who would agree with you," Bat replied. "But those same people would also say that I'm honest."

From those who had gathered around to watch the drama play out before them, laughter broke out along with a spattering of applause for Bat's words.

"Now, if you gentlemen will excuse me, I intend to buy a new shirt and a new pair of trousers with my honestly earned funds," Bat said.

"Ha, you'd spend your money on fancy duds," Ed said. "I'm going down to the Dodge House and have a fine meal."

"The Dodge House? Is that a new place?" Theo asked.

"Just another name change," Ed said. "Mr. Cox has a new partner, and Mr. Boyd wants a new name."

"Well, then let's all go try out the Dodge House," Theo said.

"Cade?" Ed invited. "Are you going with us?"

"I'd rather not."

Chapter Fourteen

CADE WAS playing cards at Hoodoo Brown's place, when a shadow fell across the table. Looking up, he saw Jacob Harrison.

"Jacob!" he said, grinning broadly. Standing, he extended his hand.

"Hello, Cade. I was told I might find you here."

Cade and Jacob had done some freighting business together in the recent past. It was that experience that Cade had used as a means of searching for Arabella, but it had been almost a year since he had last seen Jacob.

"If you aren't a sight for sore eyes. What are you doing here, in Dodge?" Cade asked. "The last I heard you were working out of Hays City."

"I have been, but I've got a new contract with the army."

"What sort of contract?"

"Freighting, same as before. Now that the railroad's here, Fort Dodge will be an even bigger shipping point that it has been before," Jacob said. "I'll be hauling supplies down to Camp Supply and Fort Reno."

"And you need a driver," Cade said. He smiled. "Yes, I'll be glad to drive for you."

"I don't need a driver," Jacob said.

"Oh, I'm sorry, I just assumed that . . ."

"What I need is a partner."

"A partner?" Cade shook his head. "Jacob, you know I'd like nothing better than to become your partner, but I don't have any money to put into the business. Like I said, I'd be glad to be one of your drivers, though."

"No, I want more than that. I want you as a full and equal partner."

"You don't understand the situation," Cade said.

"If you mean about you and Jeter losing the Red House, yes, I am aware of that."

Cade shook his head. "Jeter had nothing to do with it. I managed to lose it all by myself, and now I'm absolutely broke. Jacob."

"Look, the first run will pay us seven hundred and fifty dollars," Jacob said. "Right now, I've got five hundred dollars invested in stock and three wagons. If we split the take, fifty-fity, you can give me two hundred and fifty dollars from your share to cover my expenses, that'll make you a full partner, and you'll still have a little money left over. What do you say?"

Cade grinned again, and extended his hand. "You don't know how much I need this right now. I'd say you have yourself a partner."

Lola Fontaine had been sitting at one of the tables nearest the front window of the Devil's Den when she saw three wagons with the name Harrison and McCall Freight Company blazoned on the side board. She saw Cade McCall sitting in the front wagon, and she recalled her visit with him. He had not come back into the Devil' Den since that one visit, and in truth, she was glad he had not. She had been wrestling with the truth as she knew it, but now that McCall was moving on with a new business, it would make it easier to keep quiet.

The Devil's Den was a rough place, but in her current position, she was out of the fray. The girls she had hired were making more money, and to Luke and Mack's credit, they didn't let the men abuse them.

"Lola," Luke said, coming over to sit with her. "I need to talk to you about one of your girls."

"Oh? Is someone giving you trouble?"

"No, it's not that. It's the young one. I think you call her Cetti."

"I know she doesn't bring in any money, but we need someone to do the laundry."

"It's not what she costs me," Luke said. "It's just that mor'n one of the customers has asked about her. As young and fresh as she is, why the one that would bust her in would pay a pretty penny to be the first one."

"No, Luke, Cetti's not going to whore for you."

"Why not? It ain't like she don't know what's goin' on here. Why her own sister is whorin'. And, if we was to start usin' her, she'd make two or three times as much as any of the other girls."

Lola shook her head. "No, Luke, when I hired Frankie, I promised her I'd look out for Cetti. In a couple more years, if Cetti decides she wants to go into the business, it'll be her own idea. Right now she's too young."

"How old was you, when you started out?" Luke asked

Lola flashed an enigmatic smile. "That, Mr. Slater, is none of your business."

"Tell me, Miss Lola, do you like your job?"

"I do."

"Well you're going to have to make a decision and it'll be real soon. Either that little girlie goes on the line, or you go back on your back," Luke said. "Do you understand what I'm saying?"

Lola remained silent as Luke turned and walked away, the anger evident in his stride.

The Harrison and McCall wagons had just passed the Odee Road Ranch, and so far there had been no significant troubles. One of the mules had slipped out of his tether one night and rounding him up had slowed them down for an hour or so, but other than that, Jacob and Cade were enjoying reconnecting with one another.

"Jeter still hasn't come around?" Jacob asked.

"Can you blame him?"

"I don't know, you two have been friends for a long time. I know that friends sometimes have a falling out, but generally the friendship is strong enough to overcome it."

"This is more than a falling out. I took his livelihood away from him."

"It isn't as if you did it on purpose."

"No, I did it while I was drunk, and that's just as bad."

"Well, you're sober now," Jacob said. "And you'll do no good by kicking yourself for past transgressions. The best thing for you to do now is to look to the future."

"The future is what I dread most. I don't know if Jeter ever will get over this. What's worse, I don't know if I can ever forgive myself, not only for what I did to Jeter...but for what I have done to Chantal, from the very moment she was born. I made a vow to Arabella, on her deathbed, mind you. And I have broken that vow."

"Have a little faith, Cade. You are not beyond redemption, trust me."

Just ahead of the approaching wagons, an Indian was on top of a ridge, looking down at the road below. He was lying just behind the crest of the ridge so he could not be seen in silhouette. When he saw the approaching wagons, he wriggled back down to a point where he could stand and return to the ten warriors who waited by their horses.

"White men come with their wagons," he said, holding up three fingers. "We will steal the mules and take what they carry."

Waquini mounted his horse and led the others to a curve in the road. He felt a sense of power, in that the warriors were following him. He was not a chief, but he had convinced the others that he could communicate directly with the Great Spirit. He said that those who would ride with him would be protected from the white man's bullets, and the ten men who followed him, did so with absolute confidence.

As they waited, Waquini saw a skunk's tail hanging from the harness of one of the others.

"No!" he said. He pointed to the skunk. "You have killed my totem! You have broken my power for this raid!"

"They are here!" one of the other Indians shouted, and with a loud whoop, he started toward the approaching wagons.

"No!" Waquini called to them, but it was too late.

"Damn!" Cade shouted. "We've got company!"

Even as Cade gave the warning he was lifting a Winchester to his shoulder and firing in almost the same motion. The lead Indian, who was charging the wagons with a raised war-club, tumbled from his saddle.

The other Indians in the war-party were less dependent on the traditional Indian weapons, and they were well equipped with rifles of their own. The Indians began firing at the men on the wagons. Cade brought down a second Indian. By now Jacob had stopped the wagon and picked up his own rifle. A third Indian went down from his shot, and two more Indians were dropped by the others of the wagon team. Now, only four Indians remained, and seeing that they were suddenly outnumbered by the six men on the wagons, they turned and rode away, leaving their dead behind.

"Was anyone hurt?" Cade called back to the others.

"Nobody hit here," the driver of the second wagon replied.

"We're all right back here," the third driver called.

"I wonder how many more there are?" Jacob asked.

"I don't know. But we'd better get out of here," Cade said.

"I think you're right," Jacob said. "Let's move on out."

When the last wagon started to move, one of drivers called out.

"We can't go, we've got a mule hit back here!"

"Whoa," Jacob said, pulling the team to a halt.

Cade and Jacob climbed down then walked back to the third wagon where they saw Foster and Keaton looking at the mule. It was braying loudly and they discovered she had been hit in the side and was bleeding badly.

"We'd better get her disconnected as fast as we can," Jacob said when he got back to her. "This mule's about to die, and if she falls in place, we'll have one hell of a time getting the wagon moved around her."

"You know what, the Indians didn't recover any of their dead, and they may decide to come back," Cade said. "Maybe we'd better put the other two wagons in a defensive position, in case they try to hit us again."

"All right, do it," Jacob agreed.

"Are we gonna have to put her down?" Foster asked.

"I'm afraid so."

"Damn, I hate that. Maude's a good old mule."

"I'm sorry girl," Jacob said soothingly, to the mule that was hit. He began stroking her on the forehead, and she dipped her head several times, then put her head against his chest.

Cade watched for a minute, feeling an intense sadness. Then he considered their situation.

"I think I'd better go on up ahead and keep a lookout," Cade said.

When Waquini returned to the village it was quickly noticed that there were six fewer warriors with him now, than there had been when he left.

"You were wrong to lead a war party," Spotted Wolf scolded. "We are at peace with the white man, but you made war and now there will be weeping among the women for those who were killed."

"Waquini lied," one of the Indians who had gone with him said. He pointed to the medicine man and shouted, "You said you could protect us from the White Man's bullets, but many were killed!"

"It is your fault!" Waquini said. He pointed to the skunk tail that hung from the warrior's harness. "Did I not tell you that you have killed my totem? Did I not say that we should not attack?"

"He speaks the truth," one of the others from the raiding party said. "Waquini did tell us not to attack."

"My medicine is strong," Waquini said. "But in order for it to be true, I must do nothing to anger the spirits. The spirit of the skunk gives me the power to protect my people from the enemy. When the skunk is killed by one who would follow me, that spirit is broken."

"Where are the white men you attacked?" Spotted Wolf asked.

"They cower on the road where the fight was."

"And the warriors who didn't come back? Where are they?" Spotted Wolf asked.

Waquini didn't answer.

"Do they sleep on the road near the white men?"

"Yes," the Indian who had the killed the skunk replied.

"I will go and bring them back."

"You cannot go," Waquini said. "My power has been broken."

"My power has not been broken," Spotted Wolf replied.

The wagons had remained in place for just over an hour, and Cade glanced back a few times. He saw Maude lying on the ground, well off the side of the road, but he hadn't heard the gunshot yet, and he knew why. Everyone was hoping that Maude would die on her own, because nobody wanted to pull the trigger. Then Jacob waved to him, and he started back, but he glanced down the road one more time before he left the ridge.

What he saw caused him to gasp in surprise. He saw a single Indian coming up the road, leading three rider-less horses. The Indian was making no effort to conceal himself.

"I'll be damn," Jacob said under his breath. "I'll say this for you. You are one courageous son of a bitch."

Cade waited until the Indian was practically even with him, then he stood up and, called out to him.

"Hold it right there, Indian!" he shouted. Though he didn't raise the rifle to his shoulder, he held it in positon to do so, quickly, if need be.

The Indian stopped, and held up his hand. Cade saw, then, that there was a travois behind each of the horses.

Cade looked down the road in the direction from which the Indian had come. The road was clear for at least a mile back, and there were no ridge lines adjacent to the road that would have provided concealment for any Indians who might have come with him.

Cade ambled down the hill until he was within a few feet of the Indian. From as much as he could tell, the Indian was unarmed.

"I am Spotted Wolf," the Indian said.

"What do you want, Spotted Wolf?"

"I have come for those who sleep."

"You mean the ones we killed today? The ones who were trying to kill us?"

"I was not with the war party," Spotted Wolf said.

As Cade made a closer examination of the Indian, he saw that he was considerably older than any of those who had attacked them. If he had to guess, he would say that Spotted Wolf was in his mid to late seventies.

"Why should I let you have them?" Cade asked.

"I will protect you. You will reach the place of the soldiers."

"You will protect us?"

"Yes."

"How are you going to do that all by yourself?"

"I am Spotted Wolf," the Indian repeated, as if that was all the validation his claim needed.

Cade made another perusal of the area, and seeing no more Indians, lowered the rifle.

"Wait here," he said. "I'll go ahead and tell the others you're coming."

With the six dead Indians loaded onto the travois, Spotted Wolf led the wagons farther south.

121

"We're damn near to Camp Supply now," Jacob said. "It's not more than another couple of miles. Surely he's not going to take us all the way to the gate."

As if Spotted Wolf had heard Jacob speak, the Indian dropped the reins of the three horses he was leading, then rode back to the wagon.

"I go now," he said.

"Wait," Cade said. Reaching back into the wagon he picked up a bag of coffee and a side of bacon. "This is for you," he said, handing the two items to the Indian.

Spotted Wolf smiled at the unexpected gifts, but said nothing. Instead, he returned to the three horses, who had remained motionless, picked up the reins, then left the road, riding west across the gently rolling hills.

Chapter Fifteen

OVER THE NEXT few months buffalo hides and the railroad turned Dodge City into a boomtown. The town's charter members were able to make money by selling off lots at fifty dollars apiece, and the merchants of the town, such as Charles Rath and Robert Wright, Herman Fringer, and George Hoover, were making a lot of money off the buffalo trade. Frederick Zimmermann, a gunsmith who had learned his trade in Europe, was doing a booming business in his hardware store, his biggest business coming from the sale of firearms and ammunition. It was said he was selling between fifty and seventy-five guns a week, and that he ordered cartridges in lots of seventy-five thousand to keep up with the demand.

Although Cade and Jacob had thought the coming of the railroad would diminish their business, it had proved just the opposite. Business was booming for them as well, and a couple of times Cade had tried to approach Jeter to invite him to join the company. Jeter wouldn't even talk to him, and when he sent Jacob to speak on his behalf, Jeter turned him down cold.

The winter saw an increase in business for Harrison and McCall, as the buffalo hunters were out in force, taking the buffalo with the best robes. They also continued their contracts with the army, hauling supplies from Fort Dodge and Fort Larned in Kansas, to Camp Supply, Fort Reno, and even Fort Sill in the Indian Territory. During the winter they added more Studebaker wagons and more muleskinners to drive them as they provided much needed supplies to the Indian agencies, both the Kiowa-Comanche, and the Cheyenne-Arapaho Agency.

"How John!" Spotted Wolf greeted Cade and Jacob when they pulled into the Cheyenne Village with bacon, flour, sugar, and coffee. "How John" was Spotted Wolf's normal greeting.

"Hello, Spotted Wolf," Cade replied, raising his own hand. "We brought you some supplies."

"Any bullets? Spotted Wolf asked. "Any rifles?"

Cade shook his head. "I'm afraid not. Just food."

"We need rifles and bullets to hunt buffalo."

"We've got a whole wagon load of food for you," Cade said with a cheerful smile.

"We thank you for that," Spotted Wolf said.

"We are not children to be fed," another Indian said, gruffly.

"Who is the ingrate?" Jacob asked.

"I do not understand the word," Spotted Wolf replied.

"The Indian who does not thank us," Cade explained, pointing to the scowling Indian. "Who is he?"

"That is Waquini. It means nose that does not run straight," Spotted Wolf added, laying a finger aside his own nose to demonstrate.

Cade looked at the Indian, and though he had seen broken noses before, he had never seen a nose as crooked as this one.

"It sure as hell doesn't run straight," Cade said with a little laugh.

"It is a noble name," Waquini insisted.

"You're right, Waquini, and I apologize for laughing."

"Do you apologize for killing my brothers?" Waquini asked.

"When did I kill your brothers?"

"In the time of the red and yellow leaves," Spotted Wolf said. "It was Waquini who led the war party against your wagons."

"That was you, and you want me to apologize? Hell no, I'm not going to apologize. You killed my mule, and besides that, you attacked me, I didn't attack you."

So quickly that he didn't even see it until it happened, Waquini threw a knife that stuck into the ground but inches in front of Cade's feet.

Spotted Wolf said several angry words to Waquini, who responded just as angrily. Waquini pointed to Cade, and even though Cade couldn't understand the language, he was fairly certain he knew what Waquini was saying.

"He wants to fight you, Cade," Jacob, who also understood the intent, said. "That son of a bitch actually wants to fight you."

"Yeah, that's the way I see it."

"These white eyes are our friends," Spotted Wolf said to Waquini, speaking in English now so that Cade and

Jacob could understand what he was saying. "They have brought food so that our women and children will not starve during the time of snow."

"If there were no white men to kill the buffalo, if there were no white men to drive us from our own lands, we would not need for them to feed us as if we are children," Waquini replied, also speaking in English. He pointed to the knife he had thrown.

"Pick up the knife, white eyes. Pick up the knife and fight me, if you are not a coward."

Cade started toward the knife, but Spotted Wolf spoke up. "If you do not wish to fight Waquini, I will stop him."

"No, I'll fight him."

"Don't do it, Cade," Jacob said. "This son of a bitch has probably been fighting with a knife ever since he was ten years old. And what if you win, and you kill him? Even with Spotted Wolf on our side, we would be lucky if we made it out of here alive."

"I'm going to fight him," Cade said, as he picked up the knife.

Waquini began shouting, singing, and dancing, keeping it up for at least thirty seconds.

"Spotted Wolf, does he want to fight or not?" Cade said, moving his hand toward the howling, dancing, Indian.

"He is doing his death dance," Spotted Wolf said.

"Ha! Well, I must say, his lack of self-assurance gives me a little more confidence."

Suddenly, and with no forewarning, Waquini made a sweep toward Cade, his arm lashing out as if it had been a part of the dance. Cade leaped back from the flashing blade, doing so barely in time to avoid being disemboweled. But he didn't get back quickly enough to avoid all injury, for the point of the blade cut through the flannel shirt Cade was wearing, and opened up a cut across his stomach.

Although the cut was shallow, it was deep enough to spill blood and, instantly, the front of Cade's shirt began to stain red. Waquini misinterpreted the effectiveness of his slash and moved in for what he assumed would be the kill. To his surprise, Cade was able to skip to the side, avoiding the thrust, and countering with his own slashing move. He managed to spill some of the Indian's blood, but the overall effectiveness of Cade's stroke was of no greater consequence than Waquini's had been a moment earlier.

There were no surprises remaining between the two men. They thrust and counter-thrust, drawing nothing but empty air with each attempt. By now several of the villagers had gathered, making a large circle around the two fighting men. No advantage accrued to either fighter until Waquini made one longer than normal thrust with his knife. The effect pulled Waquini off balance, and he stumbled forward. Cade took advantage of the situation by hooking his foot behind Waquini's knee, and sweeping Waquini's leg out from under him.

Waquini went down, dropping his knife as he did so. Quickly, Cade kicked the knife away, then he dropped down on Waquini's prostrate form, putting his knee on Waquini's chest, and placing the point of his knife at the jugular vein on the Indian's neck.

"One half inch, and you'll be a dead Indian," Cade said.

Waquini spit in Cade's face, and to the amazement of everyone, Cade laughed.

Cade got up, threw the knife so that it stabbed into the ground, then extended his hand in an offer to help Waquini to his feet.

"No!" Waquini shouted, as if he had just been hit. He rolled over quickly, stood, then without looking at Cade, walked away quickly.

Cade watched Waquini hurry off. Then he saw that several of the Indians who had watched the fight turned their backs on the departing Indian.

"What is it? What did I do wrong?" Cade asked.

"You should have killed the son of a bitch, Cade," Jacob said. "You didn't and that's your mistake."

"Why should I have killed him? The fight was over; I was no longer in any danger. There was no need to kill him," Cade said.

"You don't understand," Jacob explained. "If you had killed him, he could have died with honor. But you spared him, and now he must live with shame."

Cade shook his head. "I thought that by sparing him, I could make a friend of him."

"I'm afraid that all you have done is make a terrible enemy," Jacob replied.

Cade rubbed his hands together, then walked back toward the wagon. "Yeah, well, apparently he was already a bitter enemy. The first thing he tried to do when he saw me, was kill me."

"Yes, but that was a fair fight, where he could win honor by killing you," Jacob said. "Now, the only thing he can do to take away the dishonor you have shown him, is kill you."

"He tried it once; if he wants another try at it, I'll face him down again," Cade said.

"You don't understand. He doesn't have to face you down. All he has to do is kill you."

"Where's the honor in that?"

"There is no honor in it," Jacob replied. "But since you shamed him by sparing his life, there will be no dishonor in killing you any way he can."

On the far side of the village, Cade saw Waquini mount his horse, then ride away.

"You mean I'm going to have to look over my shoulder for that son of a bitch from now on?"

"I'm afraid so," Jacob said.

"For how long?"

"Until one of you is dead."

"Damn, I should have killed him when I had a chance," Cade said.

Jacob smiled. "That you should have, my friend."

As Dodge City was growing, it was acquiring the unwanted reputation of being a lawless and violent town. With the increase of population came even more gamblers, whores, and desperados who were drawn to a town that had no law. And because there was no law in Dodge City, every merchant, and even the clerks who worked in the stores, were armed, due to the fact that they could be robbed at any time.

Though the citizens of the town, as well as the legitimate businesses, were troubled by this influx of undesirables, the saloons fared well. Even so, there was a shooting in one of the saloons on a near weekly basis, and the saloon that was doing the most business, and which was experiencing the most violence, was the Devil's Den. Only the Dodge House, of all the saloons in town, was able to maintain a degree of decorum.

Magnolia, who was the chef at the Dodge House, was in Evans' grocery store buying for the Dodge House, when a young black soldier came in. Billy Taylor was a cook for Colonel Dodge, the commanding officer of Fort Dodge, the similarity in his name and the name of the fort being just a coincidence.

"*Bonjour, Monsieur* Taylor," Magnolia said, greeting him with a smile.

"Miz Willis," Taylor replied, touching his eyebrow in a salute.

"I guess you and I are doing the same thing this morning, trying to decide what we're going to cook today," Magnolia said.

"Yes, ma'am, though I 'spects your cookin' will be finer 'n my cookin'."

"Oh, don't sell yourself short, *Monsieur*. I've been told that you're a fine cook."

A proud smile spread across Taylor's face. "Yes ma'am, leastwise that's what the colonel says."

The only other customer in the store at the moment was Weasel Slater, and he watched the interplay between Magnolia, and Billy Taylor with obvious displeasure.

"Hey, Evans, what's that black bastard doin' in here? This here store is for whites only," Weasel said

"You're wrong, Slater," Richard Evans replied. "This store is for anyone who has the money to make a purchase, and the commandant's cook fills that bill. Colonel Dodge and Private Taylor are valued customers."

"Yeah? Well, he ain't shoppin' now, is he? What he's doin' now is talkin' to a white woman, 'n he ain't got no business talkin' to her. You," Slater shouted, pointing toward Magnolia. "Get away from that man. Ain't you got no shame?"

Magnolia looked with obvious loathing at the man who had once held her and family hostage. "*Monsieur* Slater, I will talk with whomever I please," she replied.

"Oh, I get it now. Since you 'n your husband lost your saloon, you've gone into whorin', is that it? Well, you don' have to sell yourself to no black soldier. Why don't you come over 'n whore for us? That way, the only people you'll have to spread your legs for is white men. 'N me 'n my brothers, of course. We got to try out the merchandise, don't you see?" he added with an evil smirk."

"That's enough, Slater!" the storekeeper said. During Weasel's rant, Evans had taken a shotgun from under the counter. "You get out of here, now and don't come back."

"Oh, you don't have to worry none 'bout that. I don' plan to do no business with anyone who would let trash like this in their store."

"Now, Slater," Evans said, raising the shotgun to his shoulder.

Weasel walked out of the store, slamming the door behind him.

"I'm sorry about that, Mrs. Willis, Private Taylor," Evans said. "The thing is that, right now, the town's full of trash like that."

"Why, there's no need for you to apologize, *Monsieur* Evans. You handled it beautifully."

"Yes, sir, I thank you for takin' up for me like that," Taylor said.

"Come, *Monsieur* Taylor, let's put our heads together and decide what we shall cook tonight," Magnolia invited. "You for the colonel, and I for the Dodge House."

"Yes, ma'am!" Taylor answered, proudly.

"I got some apples in, yesterday," Evans said. "They'd make a mighty fine pie."

"That's a wonderful suggestion," Magnolia agreed.

"Yes, sir," Taylor said. "The colonel's got a particular likin' for apple pie."

Chapter Sixteen

WHEN WEASEL Slater stepped out into the street, he was still seething in anger over what had just happened. That's when he saw three men coming out of the Devil's Den. The three were obviously drunk, and they came across the street to greet him.

"What happened to you, Weasel?" Curly Sheldrake asked. Of the three, Curly, who had ridden on a couple of horse thieving raids a while back, was the only one that Weasel recognized.

"One minute you was behind the bar, servin' drinks, 'n the next minute you had plum disappeared on us."

"Yeah," one of the others said. "We thought you'd gone upstairs with Cetti."

"She's too young."

"What do you mean, too young? Ain't you seen how that little girl is all tittied up?"

"She's too young," Weasel repeated. "What I come over here for was to buy me some tobacco, only," he paused and pointed back toward the store, "they's one of them uppity blacks from the fort in there, 'n he's talkin' to a white woman."

"How come you just left 'im there without don' nothin' about it?" Curly asked.

"On account of Evans pulled his shotgun on me, that's why."

"And you hightailed it outta there?"

"Didn't you hear me? He was holdin' a shotgun."

"Yeah, well, that don't mean we got to let that black bastard get away with it," Curly said. "Ain't that why we fought the war?"

"What do you mean?" Weasel asked.

"Is this here his wagon, do you think?"

The wagon, with US Army markings, was parked in front of the store.

"I reckon it is, seein' as it's got army wrote on it," Weasel said.

"What do you think the army would do to that soldier boy, iffen somethin' was to happen to his wagon?" Curly asked.

"Like what would happen to it?" Weasel asked.

There was an axe and a shovel tied to the side of the wagon, and Curly untied the axe, then held it over the side of the wagon. "Like, if it was to get all chopped up," he shouted, as he brought the ax down against the front wheel, severing one of the spokes. Another chop cut through another spoke.

"Yee ha! Give it hell, Curly!" one of the other two men whooped.

By now the team of mules which were attached to the wagon began braying in fear and confusion.

"Private Taylor, is that your mules raising a fuss?" Evans asked.

"It sure sounds like it," Taylor replied. "You have a good day, Miz Willis.'"

Just as Taylor reached the front porch, the right front wheel on the army wagon had been so weakened that it could no longer support the wagon's weight, and it collapsed.

"No, what are you doing? Stop that!" Taylor shouted, and stepping down from the porch just as Curly raised the axe over his head to start on the hind wheel. Taylor jerked the axe from Curly's hands.

"Drop that axe, Taylor!" Weasel shouted as he drew his pistol.

Taylor turned to look at him. "Didn't you see him? He was bustin' up my wagon!"

Weasel pulled the trigger, and Taylor gasped, then clapped his hands over the hole in his chest. Looking down at himself, he saw bright red blood spilling between his fingers.

"Lord a' mercy, Weasel, you shot 'im!" Curly shouted.

"Shot 'im hell! He kilt 'im is what he done," one of the others said, as Taylor fell lifeless to the ground.

"I had no choice," Weasel replied. "He was comin' at me with that axe."

"Oh!" Magnolia said from the porch behind the grizzly scene. She had come outside to check on the commotion, arriving just in time to see Billy Taylor shot. *"Vous avez commis un meurtre, monsieur Slater!* You have committed murder!"

"The hell I did!" Weasel replied. "He had a axe. He was fixin' to kill me 'n would a' done it too, if I hadn't shot 'im."

"Yeah," one of the others said. "That's how it was, all right."

"It was murder, pure and simple," Jeter told the others, during an emergency meeting of the town board of directors.

"They are saying that the black soldier went after Weasel Slater with an axe," Lyman Shaw said.

"Who's saying that?" Jeter asked.

"There were three witnesses, and they're all saying that," Shaw said

"One of the . . . witnesses . . . had just chopped the front wheel off Taylor's wagon," Jeter said angrily. "How reliable are they? I'm telling you that my wife saw it, and she said all Taylor did was jerk the axe out of Curly Sheldrake's hand."

"Yeah, well, maybe Slater thought Taylor was coming after him," Robert Wright said. "If he thought that, then the killing is still justifiable as self-defense."

"It doesn't matter whether it was justifiable or not," Herman Fringer said. "We don't have any law in Dodge City, so there's nothin' we could do about it, anyway."

"Colonel, all 'n hell Taylor done was jerk the axe outta that feller's hand to keep 'im from bustin' up the wagon any more'n he already done," Sergeant Haverkost said. Haverkost had been in Dodge City when the incident occurred. "That feller, Slater, shot 'im dead for no reason a' tall that I can see."

"Has Slater been arrested?" Colonel Dodge asked.

"No, sir, he ain't been arrested on account of there still ain't no law in Dodge City."

"Then we'll provide the law," Colonel Dodge said. "Tell Captain Kirby I want to see him. Have him get his troopers ready to ride at first light."

"Cap'n Kirby, sir? He's in command of the black troops."

"Yes, I think it would be a fitting conclusion to this affair to have black soldiers arrest the murderer of a black soldier."

"Yes, sir," Sergeant Haverkost said, a grin crossing his face. "Yes, sir, I think that would be real sweet justice."

Tom Nixon, a buffalo hunter, was at the sutler's store when Sergeant Haverkost came in.

"Have you heard?" Haverkost asked the sutler. "Colonel Dodge is sending Cap'n Kirby 'n his black trooper into Dodge City to clean it up."

"What are ya a' saying?" the sutler asked.

"You knowed Private Taylor was kilt. And there was folks who seen it. They's a sayin' it was murder, plain as day."

"You don't say."

"Hell, Dodge City ain't nothin' but a hell hole anyway. If you ask me, it's about time we done somethin'. I think it's time we showed them feather merchants in a thing or two."

"When are they goin'?" the sutler asked.

"Tomorrow mornin', I think."

Nixon left the sutler store without comment, and rode at a gallop into town. By the time he pulled up in front of Rath and Company, his horse had worked up a lather.

Charles Rath was out front of his store when Nixon dismounted.

"Here, Tom," Rath said. "What's got you all excited, that you would treat your horse like that?"

"They're goin' to burn the town down," Nixon said.

"Who's going to burn the town down? If it's Indians coming, we need to get word out to the fort."

"No!" Tom said. "It's not Indians. It's the soldiers that are going to do it."

***

The Harrison and McCall Freight Company Office was across the tracks from Front Street, right next door to Cutler and Wiley's Railroad Company store. Cade and Jacob were returning with a load of flint buffalo skins after they had dropped off their delivery to Camp Supply, when they were hailed by Michael Cutler.

"Did you have a good trip?" Cutler asked.

"Yes, nobody attacked us, and we didn't have any trouble with the wagon," Cade replied. "In my book, that's a good trip."

"If you just got back, you probably haven't heard the news then, have you?" Cutler asked.

"What news" Cade asked.

"According to Tom Nixon, there's a bunch of black soldiers from the fort who plan on burning the town down."

"Tom said that? And he was sober."

"That's what he's sayin'. He heard Sergeant Haverkost tellin' the sutler," Cutler replied. "It's a big mess. Weasel Slater killed a black soldier, and it looks like the black troopers are out for revenge. Anyway, Robert Wright's called a meeting of all the town businessmen to discuss it."

"What do you think, Cade?" Jacob asked.

"Well, we're businessmen," Cade replied. "I think we should go find out what's going on."

"All right," Jacob agreed.

As the two walked from the freight office they saw Jeter ahead of them. Cade halted for a moment. "Looks like Jeter's going to be there," Cade said.

"Do you want to skip this?"

"No," Cade said. "If we're going to live in the same town, I can't avoid him for the rest of my life. Heaven knows, I've tried to make amends, but he won't accept my olive branch. The next move is up to him."

They listened to Tom Nixon's report in which he made the claim that black soldiers were coming from the fort, with orders to burn the town down in revenge for one of their own being killed.

"How do you know this?" Jeter asked.

"They're all 'em talkin' about it," Nixon replied. "The whole fort is in an uproar."

"They've got a right to be upset," Jeter said. "When Slater shot Taylor, that was nothing but pure murder."

"Jeter, we've talked about this," Wright said. "If that black trooper had an axe in his hand, then shooting him was an act of self-defense."

"It was murder," Jeter insisted.

"We know how you feel about the Slaters," James Kelley said. "And I can't say as how I blame you. If they took my saloon away from me, I'd feel the same way."

"They're not the ones who took my saloon away from me," Jeter said, glaring across the room at Cade. Cade met his gaze, but said nothing.

"Maybe so," Kelley said. James Kelley, like everyone else in town, knew the story of how Cade gambled the saloon away.

"But you have to put your own feelings aside and think of the whole town," Bob Wright said. "We can't stand by and let a mob come in here and burn us down."

"I don't see how these soldiers could do this anyway," Jeter said. "You're talking about the army here. They would have to follow the law, wouldn't they?"

"What law?" Herman Fringer asked. "That's one of our problems. We don't have any law."

"I can stop 'em," Nixon said.

"How?" Rath asked.

"There's at least thirty-five or forty buffalo hunters in town right now, all of 'em good shots, 'n all of 'em has a Sharps fifty. Why, we could wait outside town until they got here, 'n kill ever' damn one of 'em."

"No!" Cade said, speaking up, quickly.

"So, what do you say, McCall?" Nixon challenged. "You think we should just let 'em burn the place down?"

"I say go ahead and gather up the men," Cade said. "But we aren't going to ambush them. We'll meet the soldiers at the edge of town. I don't think they want to go to war with us."

"I agree with Cade," Bat Masterson said. "I'll join the group."

The next morning forty-two citizens and residents of Dodge City were one mile east of town, spread out across the road that led from Fort Dodge. Most of the members of the "Dodge City Brigade" as they were calling themselves, weren't permanent residents of the town, but were buffalo hunters. Cade, Bat Masterson, Billy Brooks, and Jeter Willis were also with the group. Jeter maintained as much of a separation between him and Cade as was possible.

By mutual agreement, Tom Nixon was in charge of the brigade, and he had advanced about a quarter of mile down the road from the others. After a short while he came back, his horse not galloping, but moving at a rapid trot.

"Here they come, boys, get ready," he said. Dismounting, he took his horse back to a place of relative safety, then he returned to his position in front of the others.

They could hear the approaching troops before they saw them, a distant rumble of hooves. They saw a cloud of dust, then mounted soldiers materialized from the dust. The soldiers were black, but the three officers leading them were white. The officer in the very front was Captain Doyne Kirby.

"Hold your guns up like this," Nixon ordered, "with the butt of the rifle on your hip."

As the soldiers approached, it was obvious that Kirby saw the men arrayed across the road in front of him. He held up his hand.

"Troop, halt!"

By now there was less than a twenty-yard separation between the soldiers and the men of the town,

"Who's in charge here?" Captain Kirby called out.

"I am," Nixon replied.

"I know you," Kirby said. "I've seen you on the post several times. You're that buffalo hunter, Billy Nixon, aren't you?"

"The name's Tom Nixon."

"What's the meaning of this, Mr. Nixon? Why are there armed men here, impeding the progress of the United States Army?"

"We ain't a' plannin' on lettin' you come into town 'n burn us out," Nixon said.

"Who gave you that idea?" Captain Kirby asked. "We have no intention of burning anyone out. All we intend to do is go into town, arrest this . . . Weasel Slater, I believe his name is, and bring him back to the fort for trial for the murder of Trooper Taylor."

"We ain't goin' to let you do that, neither," Nixon said. "Fact is, I'm orderin' you to turn aroun' 'n go back to the post. You ain't wanted here."

"And if we refuse?"

"They's more 'n forty of us here," Nixon said, taking in the men behind him with a sweep of his arm. "Most is buffalo hunters. Ever' damn one of us has a

Sharp's fifty, 'n a hunnert rounds of ammunition. 'N I'll tell you this, right now, if we commence to shootin', you three white officers will be the first to go down. Then, we'll take all these black heathens that's behind you, down to the Arkansas River, 'n we'll drown 'em."

"I think you're bluffing," Captain Kirby said. "You wouldn't dare shoot at the United States Army."

"You'd better take heed, Captain," Cade McCall said as he moved forward. "I did a lot of shooting at the U.S. Army during the war, and I'm not the only one in the group to have done so."

Captain Kirby glared at the assembled men of Dodge City for a long time, then he held up his hand.

"Left column, left about, right column, right about!" he shouted, making a circle with his hand. The soldiers who had advanced by a column of twos, now peeled off by columns to the left and to the right, then started back in the opposite direction.

"Officers post!"

The two Lieutenants who were with him, turned and hurried to be in front of the troop as it started back toward Fort Dodge.

"We'll be back with a legal warrant to arrest the murderer," Captain Kirby said. "You can count on that."

"Yeah? Well don't bring no troop of black soldiers with you, 'cause next time we'll commence shootin', soon as we see you," Nixon said.

"Forward," Kirby ordered.

"Forward!" came the supplemental commands from the two lieutenants.

"Ho!"

Cade watched the troops withdraw, then he looked for Jeter. Jeter was already heading back to town.

Chapter Seventeen

THE NEXT DAY Colonel Dodge left the fort and proceeded to Dodge City, not with a mere handful of troops, but with most of his regiment. Posting his troops in a blocking position on the road at each end of the town, the colonel met with Robert Wright. There was no mayor of the town, but Colonel Dodge realized that for all intent and purposes, Wright filled that position.

"What can I do for you, Colonel?" Wright asked.

"I'm here to inform you that I've put a blockade on the town," Colonel Dodge said. "I intend to search for the murderer of Private Taylor, and until that search is concluded, I will not allow anyone to enter or leave Dodge City."

"You can't do that," Wright protested. "The army has no authority over civilian matters.

"Oh, but I do. I want you to read this telegram," Colonel Dodge said, handing the paper to Wright.

> *To Richard I. Dodge*
> *Colonel Comdg. Third Infantry*

Fort Dodge, Kansas

Until Ford County is fully organized you are authorized to hold, subject to orders of the civil authorities of the proper judicial districts, all persons notoriously guilty of a violation of the criminal laws of this state. I desire that you should exercise authority with great care and only in extreme cases.

Thomas A. Osborn
Governor of Kansas

"This says only in extreme cases," Wright said.

"Do you not consider the murder of my personal cook an extreme case?" Colonel Dodge asked.

"Ordinarily I would, but it shames me to say that we've had so many murders here that it would strain credulity to single out one, as extreme."

"Well, I consider the murder, by a civilian, of a soldier of the United States Army to be extreme enough to satisfy the governor's restrictions. Therefore I intend to find that murderer. I'm told that the murderer's name is Weasel Slater."

"I'm not conceding that it's murder," Wright said. "But that is the name of the man who killed the soldier."

Leaving Wright, Colonel Dodge, with a squad of armed soldiers, entered the Devil's Den.

"I'm looking for Weasel Slater," Colonel Dodge said. "I'm told he's your brother."

"He is," Luke said. "Only he ain't here no more."

"Where is he?"

145

"I don't rightly know," Luke said. "See, here's the thing. When that colored man come after him with that axe, well, Weasel didn't have no choice but to shoot 'im. He hated doin' it, I mean the colored man bein' a soldier 'n all, but what was he to do, just stand there 'n get his head bashed in?

"Anyhow, he got word that some of the other soldiers was lookin' for 'im to kill 'im, so he left town. 'N I don't blame him none neither. Why, me 'n my brother both told 'im to do that."

After hearing this, Colonel Dodge dispatched his soldiers to search the place, but found no trace of Weasel Slater. Concluding that the man was not at the Devil's Den, the colonel had all the other business establishments searched as well.

In the meantime, Cade and Jacob were supposed to pick up a load of supplies from Fort Dodge, but when they attempted to leave, they were turned back by the soldiers that were posted at the end of town.

When they came back, Cade saw Colonel Dodge standing on the porch in front of Zimmerman's Hardware. He knew the colonel fairly well, because for the last six months, he and Jacob had done a lot of business with him. He stopped the wagon in front of the store.

"Good morning, Colonel."

"Mr. McCall, Mr. Harrison," Colonel Dodge replied.

"You and your boys seem to be pretty busy right now," Cade said.

"We're looking for that son of a bitch that killed Private Taylor."

"Yes, sir, that would be Weasel Slater," Cade said. "But he isn't in town anymore."

"You know this for a fact, do you, McCall?"

"A hard, absolute fact? No, to be honest, I can't tell you that. But I'm more than just reasonably certain that he's gone. I haven't seen him around lately, and he normally makes himself pretty visible."

The Colonel shook his head. "It's a damn shame when a good man like Taylor gets shot down—is murdered— and there's no fear of legal consequences."

"Unfortunately you're right about that," Cade replied.

"McCall, how sure are you that this Weasel Slater, the man we're looking for, is gone? You said you were reasonably certain, would you go on record as being more than 'reasonably' certain?"

Cade smiled. "I'm damn certain, Colonel."

Despite the gravity of the situation, Colonel Dodge chuckled. "All right, 'damn certain' being more dogmatic than 'reasonably certain' I'll end the search, and lift the blockade."

"The town will appreciate that."

"Lieutenant Nichols!" Colonel called.

"Yes, sir?" Lieutenant Nichols was standing out in the middle of Front Street supervising the search for Weasel Slater.

"Recall the troops, Lieutenant. We're returning to the post."

"Very good, sir," Nichols replied. "Sergeant Cobb?"

"Yes, sir?"

"Recall the troops!"

Three buildings down the street from Zimmerman's Hardware, Jeter was standing in the front door of the

Dodge House Saloon. He was watching the conversation between Cade, who was still sitting in the wagon, and Colonel Dodge, who had stepped out into the street to speak with him.

"What's going on down there?" George Cox asked.

"It looks like Cade and the colonel are palaverin' about something," Jeter replied.

"I hope he's telling them to leave."

"Ha!" Pete Cahill said from behind the bar. "If that's the best man we can get to talk to the colonel, the army will be here 'til Christmas."

"There's not a better men than Cade McCall."

"What?" both Cox and Cahill asked, the response in unison.

"Jeter, this, coming from you?" Cox asked, surprised by Jeter's comment. "I thought you and McCall were on the outs."

"We are," Jeter said. "But that's a personal matter between Cade and me. And our disagreement has nothing to do with the quality of man that Cade McCall is. He's as fine a man as I've ever known."

An army sergeant stepped up to the front of Dodge House. "Any of my men in here?"

"No," Cox replied. "There were a couple of soldiers here a while ago, but they did a search of the building and satisfied themselves that Slater wasn't here, so then they left."

"What's going on, Sergeant?" Jeter asked.

"We're goin' back to the fort," the sergeant answered.

"Did you find Slater?" Cox asked.

The sergeant shook his head. "No, the skunk wasn't nowheres to be found. I think the son of a bitch done skedaddled outta here."

"That's what the colonel was told as soon as you got to town," Cox said.

"Yes sir, there was lots of folks told us that Slater was gone, but the colonel didn't listen to none of 'em 'till McCall told 'im. It seems the colonel puts some store in that feller's words."

"Well, I'm sorry you didn't find the man you were looking for," Cox said, "but I can't say I'm sorry to see you leave."

Two weeks later, after having taken a load down to the North Fork of the Canadian, Cade and Jacob reached the Cheyenne village of Spotted Wolf. By now most of the Indians in the village knew Cade and Jacob, and knew that their arrival represented a fresh supply of food, so they were greeted warmly.

In addition to the subsistence items: flour, coffee, corn and tobacco, Cade and Jacob had brought what the Indian agent had called trifling objects. These included beads and bracelets, shawls, handkerchiefs, vests, and bolts of mainly red cloth that would be traded for buffalo skins. When the wagon rolled to a stop, the Indian women soon surrounded it, digging through the items looking for the most favored item—New York umbrellas.

Spotted Wolf came to meet them as well a smile on his face. "At last you come, my friend."

"It hasn't been that long," Cade said extending his hand. "We were here about six weeks ago weren't we?"

Spotted Wolf shook his head. "Look, the women. They miss you. Come, we eat."

Spotted Wolf took them to his own teepee where his wife, Quiet Stream, had a hump of buffalo roasting over an open fire. She had wild onions charring in the coals as she made fry bread on a hot stone.

When the two men sat down with Spotted Wolf, they eagerly ate the food.

"Very good," Cade said, and even though Quiet Stream spoke no English, she knew she had been complimented, and she beamed, proudly.

"I didn't see my old . . . friend . . . Waquini," Cade said. He set the word "friend" apart from the rest of the sentence so Spotted Wolf would know that it was in jest.

"Waquini has much dishonor," Spotted Wolf said. "Waquini led five of our young on a war path that did not end well. They went to a house near the border to steal some horses, but the man had many men with him. When Waquini returned, it was without horses, and with only two others."

"I'm sorry for the loss of your young men," Cade said. "But maybe by now, if Waquini's medicine is broken, perhaps he won't be able to get any more warriors to follow him."

"Waquini believes that his medicine was broken when you took his honor," Spotted Wolf said. "He believes he cannot get it back until he has killed you."

"Damn, he still wants to kill me, huh?"

"It is how his medicine will return," Spotted Wolf said.

"Where is he now? We need to get this settled. Is he in the village?"

"When he learned you come." Spotted Wolf flung out his arm. "He go."

Chapter Eighteen

CADE AND JACOB had spent the night on Mulberry Creek about eight miles south of Dodge City, and now they were having a breakfast of biscuits, bacon, and coffee. They could have pushed on into town the night before, but if they had it would have been after midnight before they would have reached Dodge. Now, they would arrive before noon, well rested after the two weeks they had been out on the road.

"I'll be damn glad to get back," Jacob said. "If we own this outfit, why is it we're the ones out here sleeping on the ground?"

"I don't mind," Cade said.

"Of course you don't" Jacob said. "All you do is work. You should find you a good woman."

"You mean like Katherine Markley," Cade joked. "I see you going over to Charlie Rath's house all the time."

"Miss Markley is visiting her cousin, and I want her to feel welcomed in Dodge City."

"Sure you do. You just don't want her going back to Ohio."

"McCall! McCall!"

The shout came from down the road, and when they looked they saw someone galloping toward them.

"What the . . . look it's an Indian," Jacob said.

"It's Spotted Wolf!" Cade said, standing and stepping out into the road.

"Spotted Wolf, over here!" Cade shouted, waving his arms.

Spotted Wolf maintained a gallop until he reached their camp, then he leaped down. "It is Waquini!"

"Waquini?"

"Before you leave village, Waquini go away. He will wait for you and from hiding he will kill you,"

"Where do you think he is now?"

Before Spotted Wolf could respond to Cade's question, there was the crack of a rifle shot.

"Uhh!" Spotted Wolf said, as a bullet hole appeared in his left shoulder.

"Down, get down!" Cade shouted, and he pushed Spotted Wolf to the ground. Jacob needed no further encouragement; he was down as quickly as Cade and Spotted Wolf.

"Do you see him?" Cade asked.

"No," Jacob answered.

"The shot came from our left." Cade said. "He must be in that grove of trees."

There was another shot, and the bullet hit the campfire, sending up a little shower of sparks. This time Cade saw the puff of smoke, and he had Waquini located.

152

"Jacob, I know where he is."

"Where?"

"I don't want him to see me point. You and Spotted Wolf get behind the wagon. That'll get you out of the line of fire."

"And what are you going to do?"

"I'm going to give Waquini his honor back."

"What?"

"Please, Jacob, just get behind the wagon, and no matter what you see, or think you see, pay no attention to it. Stay back there. He doesn't want you, he wants me."

"All right," Jacob said, reluctantly.

"Remember, don't pay any attention to what you think you see."

"I don't know what the hell you're up to."

Cade gave a small, self-deprecating chuckle. "Yeah, that's the problem. I'm not sure I know either."

Cade waited until Jacob and Spotted Wolf were safely behind the wagon.

"Waquini, you son of a bitch!" Cade shouted. "I'm coming to get your ass!"

Cade stood up, then started running toward the trees where he had seen the puff of smoke. He felt his muscles tensing, and his heart was in his throat as he realized the danger to which he was exposing himself. Then with every nerve in his body screaming, he jumped to one side, just as Waquini's rifle barked again.

"Uhhng!" Cade called out, and with his hands outstretched, he fell face down.

"Cade!" Jacob shouted. "He got him! Waquini shot him!"

Jacob started to get up, but Spotted Wolf reached out to pull him back.

"No, McCall say stay."

Waquini appeared from behind the trees, and he stared at the body lying on the ground some fifty yards in front of him. The body lay absolutely motionless.

"You are dead!" Waquini shouted. "My enemy is dead!"

Waquini began shouting and dancing as he approached the body. Then when he reached the spot where Cade was he put down his rifle and pulled his knife to take the scalp.

"Not today," Cade said, rolling over with the gun in his hand. He pulled the trigger, and a hole appeared in Waquini's forehead, just above his eyes that were open wide in shock.

"Cade! Cade, were you hit?" Jacob shouted, jumping up from the wagon and running toward him.

Cade laughed. "I told you not to pay any attention to whatever you thought you saw."

While Cade and Jacob were standing there, looking down at Waquini's body, Spotted Wolf came up to join them. Spotted Wolf was holding his hand over the bullet wound in his shoulder.

"He died with honor," Spotted Wolf said. "His spirit will be happy."

"Let's get the team in harness," Cade said. "We need to get Spotted Wolf to the fort and see what the doc can do to get him fixed up."

"Doc Tremaine's not there. Remember he's at Fort Leavenworth right now," Jacob said.

"Then we'll take him to the apothecary. Herman Fringer's almost as good as a doctor," Cade said. "I know he can take a bullet out because I've seen him do it."

"The wagon's pretty light right now," Jacob said. "It won't kill the mules to run them all out, at least for part of the way."

They covered the remaining eight miles in just under an hour. When they reached town they crossed the railroad on Fourth Avenue, then turned right, whereupon Cade urged the mules into a gallop for the three blocks down the street to Fringer's Drug Store.

The entry into town of a freight wagon at full gallop was unusual enough to garner the attention of the two score and more pedestrians who were going about their business. When they reached Fringer's apothecary, Cade hauled back on the reins as Jacob put his foot on the brake lever. The wagon slid to a stop, then was engulfed in the dust cloud that had been raised by its rapid passage down the dirt street.

Cade climbed out over the front wheel, then reached up to help Spotted Wolf down. The bleeding looked like it had stopped, but not before soaking Spotted Wolf's left shirtsleeve with blood.

"Hey!" someone shouted. Looking toward the man who yelled, Cade saw that it was a buffalo hunter. He saw too, by the expression on the hunter's face, that it wasn't a friendly hail.

"What's that redskin son of a bitch doin' in town? That bastard killed my sister and her family."

"How'd you know it's the same one?" another asked.

"It don't make no never mind. Theys all the same. I said I was gonna kill the next Injun I run acrost, and that'n the one."

A few more men came out of the Devil's Den, and they started moving up the street toward the drug store.

"Cade!" someone called. "In here, quick!"

Cade recognized a familiar voice and when he looked up, he saw Jeter standing there, holding the door open.

"In here!" Jeter said again, motioning to him.

Cade, Spotted Wolf and Jacob hurried across the porch and into the drugstore, managing to do so before any of the approaching men arrived. Jeter slammed and locked the door behind them, just as the mob got there. Several men began banging on the door outside.

"You sure you seen a Injun?" someone asked.

"Yeah, I'm sure."

"I didn't see no Injun."

"I see 'im," the buffalo hunter insisted.

"Turn that Injun out!" someone shouted.

"We got a rope here, we're fixin' to hang the son of a bitch!" another shouted.

"Give us the Injun!"

"You can't keep that redskin bastard in there forever!" an angry voice shouted from outside. "We'll just wait 'til you have to come out!"

"What happened to him? Did you shoot him?" Jeter asked, nodding toward Spotted Wolf.

"No," Cade answered. "He got shot saving my life. You've got to take care of him, Doc."

"I'm not a doctor, McCall," Fringer said.

"We all know that, but you're the best we've got," Jacob said. "Do whatever you can do."

"Take his shirt off," Fringer said.

"Send that redskin bastard out here!"

"We ain't a' goin' to wait all day!"

The last shout was accompanied by more banging on the door.

Spotted Wolf stripped out of his shirt and Herman Fringer put on a pair of spectacles, and examined the wound.

"It's there, but it's not too deep," Fringer said. "I should be able to get it out."

Fringer got a pan of soapy water and washed off the shoulder, disclosing a dark hole. Using a probe, he soon had the bullet out.

Spotted Wolf had no reaction to what had to be the painful digging for the bullet.

Fringer picked up a bottle of alcohol. "This is going to sting a might," he said as he poured alcohol on the wound.

Again, Spotted Wolf had no reaction.

The banging on the door got louder.

"If you don't turn that Injun sumbitch out into the street, we're goin' to come in there after 'im!"

"How much longer will that door keep them out?" Jacob asked.

"I'm afraid it's not that strong. If they decide to break it down, it'll be an easy task," Fringer said.

"Maybe we can go out through the back," Jacob suggested.

Fringer shook his head. "I don't have a back door in this place. Never did feel the need to have one."

"Well then, gentlemen, I would say that leaves us in a bit of a pickle," Jacob said.

"I know what we can do," Jeter suggested. He pointed to the wall. "I live in quarters behind the harness shop, and we share this same wall. We can go through into my place, then board up the wall behind us and nobody will know what happened."

"What about Magnolia and your ma? Won't they get scared when somebody starts tearing down the wall of their house?" Cade asked.

"When we get the first board down, I'll yell and they'll know it's me," Jeter said.

It took no more than five minutes to get enough of the boards down to allow both Jeter and Spotted Wolf to pass through. It took less time to get the boards back in place, and even the most careful observation offered no hint of what had just been done.

"What do we do now?" Fringer asked.

Cade looked at Jacob, and smiled. "You want to give up that shirt?"

"What do you mean?"

"You're the one who was wounded."

The left sleeve of Jacob's shirt was torn off, then Fringer put a bandage around his arm, just below the shoulder. Some of Spotted Wolf's blood was smeared onto the outside of the bandage.

Jacob had his hand clasped over his "wound" when three men crashed through the door.

"What the hell are you doing?" Cade asked. "The door was locked for a reason."

"Keep it as clean as you can, so that it doesn't get infected," Fringer said, loudly enough for the others to hear. "You don't want gangrene to set in."

"Thanks, Doc," Jacob replied in a strained voice.

"Here!" Luke Slater said. Luke had joined the unruly group. "What's going on here?"

"What does it look like? The doc's gone from out at the fort, and Herman here just took a bullet out of his shoulder," Cade said. "It's bad enough Jacob got shot by an Indian. He doesn't need the wound made worse by the likes of you men crowding in here."

"Where's the Injun?" the buffalo hunter who had started the demonstration demanded.

"He's lying dead just this side of Mulberry Creek. I shot him, soon as he put a bullet into Jacob," Cade said.

"You ignorant fool, I mean the Injun you brung into town. The one you was helpin' down from the wagon."

Cade shook his head. "What kind of whiskey are you serving over there, Slater? Whatever it is, it's either made this man blind, or crazy." He looked directly at the buffalo hunter. "The wounded man you saw me help down from the wagon is Jacob Harrison, and here he is."

"You're a' lyin'!" the buffalo hunter said.

Cade glared at the man. "What's your name?" he asked.

"The name's Kirk Jordan, if it's any of your business."

"Well, Mr. Jordan, when someone accuses me of lying, I make it my business. Whatever Indian you think you saw, isn't here."

"The hell he ain't! I seen 'im, I tell you."

"Are you sure 'bout that, Jordan? 'Cause you're the only one who seen 'im," Slater said.

"That ain't true," Jordan replied. He pointed to the man who had come up, first. "Wiley, he seen 'im too."

Wiley shook his head. "No, now I didn't actual see no Injun, seein' as they run into the drugstore so fast that they was gone by the time I got here."

"Gentlemen, as you can clearly see," Fringer said, "this is the wounded man McCall brought in for my attention."

"He's in here!" Jordan shouted. "That Injun sumbitch is in here someplace, on account of I seen 'im with my own eyes."

"What about we search your place, Fringer?" Wiley asked.

"You've got no right to search my business," Fringer said.

"There you go! I told you that Injun's in here. That's why he says we can't search his place."

"Well, we'll just see about that. Come on boys, let's have us a look at . . . the apothecary," Wiley said.

"No!" Fringer protested.

Despite the protest, the angry mob swarmed into the store, forcing Cade, Jacob, and Fringer out front.

"Good move, protesting like that," Cade said quietly. "When they don't find anything, they'll quit searching."

"I just hope they don't wreck the place. I've got a lot of glass in there."

A few minutes later, the men came outside.

"There ain't nobody there! Not a trace of 'im," someone shouted.

"I'm tellin' you, I seen 'im go in there!" Jordan said.

"Yeah? Well there ain't no one in there now," Wiley said. "And there ain't no way anyone could a got out."

"The Injun went out the back," Jordan insisted. "I know he did."

"He can't," Wiley said. "You seen for yourself, there ain't no back door to the place. And they don't have no window light in the back either."

"Let's leave this old coot alone," someone said. "Jordan, you owe us a drink." Grumbling, and confused, the mob returned to the Devil's Den.

Chapter Nineteen

CADE AND JACOB took the wagon back to their office, then later, when both Front Street and Tin Pot Alley were clear, Cade and Jacob went around back to knock on the door to Jeter's house. Jeter opened it with a huge smile.

"How'd it go?"

"Perfect," Cade replied. "That was a great idea you had. Oh, and thanks for letting us in the drugstore."

"I heard the wagon coming down the street on the run, and when I saw it was you, I knew you had some trouble."

"I was surprised to see you at the drug store. I thought you were working at the Dodge House."

"Ma's arthritis is kicking up a bit—it's her knee this time," Jeter said. "Herman was grinding up some powders for her."

"Do you know what's just happened here?" Jacob asked.

"What's that?" Jeter asked.

"You two. You're talking just like two normal people would talk to one another."

Jeter smiled. "I guess that's right."

"Jeter . . ." there was a long pause before Cade spoke. "Can this . . . war that's been going on between us be over?"

"Do you want it to be over?"

"Yeah, well, more than I want a stick poked in my eye," Cade replied with a broad grin.

Jeter laughed, then stuck out his hand. "All right, the war has ended. But," he added, lifting his finger. "I still reserve the right to poke you in the eye with a stick."

"Do you mind if I..." Cade started, but Jeter interrupted him in mid-sentence.

"See Chantal?"

"Yeah, I'd really like to see her."

Jeter went to a side room, and soon came out with a child that looked as if she had just been awakened. She had her arms wound around his neck.

"Here's our girl," Jeter said. "Do you want to hold her?"

Cade reached for Chantal, but she buried her head on Jeter's shoulder as she tightened her grip around his neck.

"She's not ready for her daddy, yet," Cade said. "But all that's going to change. That is if it's all right with you and Magnolia."

"It'll be good to have you come around," Jeter said. "But now don't you think we'd better get Spotted Wolf out of here?"

"I'm glad somebody thought of that while this reunion was going on," Jacob said as he patted Cade on the back. "Where is he?"

"Ma's got him hid in the other room," Jeter said. "I'll get him."

When Jeter came back, he had Spotted Wolf, who was now dressed in white man's clothing.

"Nobody saw me in the drugstore during the uproar so nobody will expect that I had anything to do with this whole thing," Jeter said. "And I've got an idea."

"Well, if it works as well as your last idea, it will be a good one."

Half an hour later Jeter showed up in the alley behind the harness shop, driving a wagon. He sent Mary outside, to see if Bridge Street was clear and to make certain no one was lurking in the alley. When Mary was satisfied that all was clear, Spotted Wolf came out, climbed into the back of the wagon, and covered himself with buffalo robes.

"Pete Cahill will meet us south of Town," Jeter said. "He'll have a horse for Spotted Wolf so he can return to his village."

Jordan had convinced some of the buffalo hunters that he had, indeed, seen an Indian coming into town, so they had put men out on the roads leading into Dodge City.

Jeter encountered Jordan himself, about half a mile south of town.

"Hold it!" Jordan said, holding up his hand. "Where do you think you're a goin', Willis?"

"I'm going out to Dugan's store," Jeter replied.

"What for?"

"I'm takin' some buffalo robes down to Dean." Jeter turned to look at the top two robes. And though he knew that these were robes that Jordan himself had brought into town, he pretended to be dumb about it.

"I just hope he'll take 'em off my hands. I'll tell you the truth, these are some of the worst robes I've ever seen. Whoever cleaned them did an awful job."

Jordan stepped up to the wagon, and recognized his mark.

"What are you talking about? These are prime robes!"

"You think so? Well, since you're a buffalo hunter, I expect you'd be a better judge of that than I am. You've made me feel better about 'em. Oh, now why was it you stopped me?"

"No reason," Jordan said, stepping out of the way. He waved his arm. "Go on, deliver your robes."

Two miles later Jeter saw Pete Cahill waiting back off the side of the road holding two horses. He motioned for him to join them.

"All right, Spotted Wolf. You can come out, now."

Spotted Wolf climbed out of the wagon.

"Do you feel up to making the long ride back to your village?" Jeter asked.

"Yes. But first I must make a travois."

"A travois? What for?"

"I will take Waquini back to our people," Spotted Wolf said.

Jeter and Cahill helped Spotted Wolf make a travois out of one of the buffalo skins, then watched as he rode away.

"Strange to think that he wants to take back the body of the same man who shot him," Cahill said.

"Indians are like that," Jeter replied. "They're just real big on honor. Come on, let's get back to town."

"What are you going to do if you get back and Jordan's still out there and he sees these same robes?" Cahill asked. "Won't he get a little suspicious?"

"You're right. Help be hide 'em in one of those ravines," Jeter said. "When all this hullabaloo blows over, I'll ride out and get them. That way it'll pay for the horse that Spotted Wolf got."

Two hours later Jeter, with Cahill riding along side, passed by the road guard, which by now had been reduced to Jordan and one other man.

"You were right," Jeter said to Jordan. "He took the robes with no question."

"I told you them was good skins," Jordan replied, waving him on through.

Chapter Twenty

ONE OF THE three wagons belonging to the Harrison and McCall Freight Company was out of commission for the moment, and it was jacked up on supports with the rear axle and wheels removed. Cade and Jacob were examining it when Jeter came out onto the wagon lot.

"So, this is your business," Jeter said, looking around.

"This is our company," Cade said proudly. "Would you like a tour?"

"Sure, why not?"

Cade took Jeter around, showing him every aspect of the business. There was a small building with the name of the company painted on a sign that was nearly as large as the space itself. Behind that building was a stock yard, with twelve mules and six horses, and there was yet another building, somewhat larger than the office building. This was the "machine shed" and here were the tools and spare parts needed to keep the wagons functioning.

"I've been curious about your operation," Jeter said. "I've wanted to come down here and take a look around."

"I'm glad you finally did."

"But, that isn't the only reason I'm here. Magnolia wants to know if you'd come over to the house for dinner tonight."

"Are you kidding me? I'd be a fool to pass up any opportunity to eat her cooking. I'll be there with bells on."

"Magnolia, that was delicious!" Cade said as he pushed away the dinner plate that evening. What was that, anyway?"

Jeter laughed. "Are you saying you didn't know it was a hen?"

Cade shook his head. "Just calling it chicken isn't enough. I know she has one of those fancy names for it."

"*Oignon de poulet*," Magnolia said with a pleased smile.

"See? Now doesn't that sound a whole lot better than calling it a chicken?" Cade asked.

Cade and Jeter moved to a settee in the corner of the room, while Magnolia and Mary washed the dishes. The two little girls, both of whom were walking and talking, were running round and round the table.

Cade watched them, feeling guilty that he had been the cause of them losing the fine house that Jeter had originally built. While this place behind the harness shop was clean, it was not a third the size of the house they had been forced to leave.

"Jeter, how much do you and Magnolia like working at the Dodge House?" Cade asked.

"It's honest employment," Jeter said, "and it keeps a roof over our head."

"I know that, and I'm not knocking it. But I've known you a long time, and I know you'd rather have something better."

"Wouldn't we all."

"I can offer that to you."

"Humph," Jeter said. He cocked his head. "Are you asking me to come work for you and Jacob?"

"No," Cade replied. "That's not what I'm asking. I'd like you to come be a full partner with Jacob and me."

"That's rich, Cade. I don't have the money to buy into any partnership, and I don't want you giving me something I didn't earn."

"That's not what I'm doing."

"Sure it is. Look, you and I have been through a very difficult time, and I'm prepared to put that behind us. But I don't want to give even the illusion that my friendship is being bought."

"That's not what I had in mind," Cade replied. "Jacob and I believe that five thousand dollars would buy one third of the company. And let's face it, you already have seventy – five hundred dollars invested in this organization."

Jeter held up his hand. "You mean the Red House. Only half of that money would be considered mine, and if you take away all the 'mistakes' Hodge Deckert has been making over the last several months when money just miraculously shows up on the books in my favor, it wouldn't even be that much."

Cade looked away. "You weren't supposed to know."

"Who else in this town would care what happened to me or to a certain little black-eyed girl?"

"All right, so you know. But back to my offer. Let's say you only have twenty-five hundred dollars invested. You'd be able to pay the rest of it within no more than three or four months and you'd still have enough money left to support your family. Are you interested?"

"I'm interested," Jeter said. "But I won't stay with it for long."

"Why not? We're making good money, and Jacob wants to get bigger."

"These trips that you take—they're from two to six weeks long, aren't they?"

"Often they are, yes," Cade said.

"Well that's the problem. I don't want to be away from Magnolia and the girls for that long, and as soon as I can put back enough money to buy another saloon, I'm going to do it," Jeter said. "Magnolia and I might open our own restaurant as well and serve all this fancy food she fixes."

"That sounds like a good plan," Cade said. He stuck out his hand. "Welcome to the company . . . partner, for however long that partnership shall be."

***

"If you ain' goin' to do any of the work, you ain' goin' to get any of the money from the Devil's Den," Luke Slater said.

"I can't stay here," Weasel replied. "There's too many soldiers come in here, you know that. 'N that damn colonel is still lookin' for me."

"Yeah, well, we didn't kill that black sonofabitch, you did," Luke said.

"What do you expect me to do? Starve to death? Hell, I ain't got no money ceptin' my share of the saloon."

"You ain't got no share o' the saloon neither," Luke insisted.

"Mack?" Weasel said, appealing to the brother who made all of the decisions for them. "Mack, do somethin'," he pleaded.

The three were sitting at a table in the back of the saloon. It was early enough in the morning that there were very few customers present, primarily because the girls, who were the principal attraction of the saloon, had not yet made their appearance, and would not until afternoon.

"He's our brother, Luke, we can't let him starve."

"Well you can give him some of your share of the money if you want to, I sure as hell ain't goin' to," Luke replied.

"Maybe it's time we expanded our business interests," Mack suggested.

"What do you mean?"

"When we were stealin' horses, one of the problems we had was that folks was always curious where we got our money. Remember over in Caldwell—anything that happened, the Slater brothers always got the blame," Mack said.

"And if we turned up with a thousand or two thousand dollars to spend, the law always got to nosin' around," Weasel said.

"Yeah, and because of that, we never could get ahead. But with the saloon . . .we'd have a place to put the money," Mack said.

"What money?" Weasel asked.

171

"The money you're going to get by going back into our old business," Mack said with a smile.

"You mean stealin' horses?"

"I see no need to limit your activities to just that."

Weasel smiled as he rubbed his hands together. "I can't wait. The three of us out together again. Why we can go all the way down to Texas and get away with it."

"No," Mack said. "That's not how it's gonna be. Luke and I will stay here and run the saloon. It'll be you who does the stealin'." Mack said.

Weasel shook his head. "No you don't. It ain't a gonna be me put my ass on the line to steal no horses. It'll be all of us a doin' this or none of us."

"Fine," Mack said. "You just told us you can't work here, 'cause of the soldiers. Well then, either you move on or you go join the other outlaws who are hidin' out skinnin' buffalo."

"I ain't gonna do that," Weasel said.

"Then round up some of the boys that was with us before, and go get some horses."

The newly formed company of Harrison, McCall and Willis had three wagons lined up, ready to head south taking lumber and supplies to the redoubt that was to be built on the Cimarron River. Cade, Jacob, and Jeter were all going on this trip, but they had hired Abe Pullen, Mike Foster and Pete Cahill to go along as helpers.

Magnolia, Mary and the girls had walked down to see the wagons roll out and they were all waving goodbye. Even though Jeter would be away no more than three weeks Magnolia felt a sense of foreboding, as if she had a premonition that something bad would happen. This was the first time the two had been separated since they had married, and Magnolia felt lost without her husband.

Magnolia wanted to get back to the house that both Cade and Jacob had helped them buy. She was glad to get away from the back of the harness shop, but the house they had bought didn't compare with the original house Jeter had built for her. The four were walking down the south side of Front Street, Chantal and Bella stopping to pick up every stick or stone or bird feather that they saw, while Mary hobbled along on her cane.

"We should have had Jeter take us home on the freight wagon," Magnolia said as they passed by a new tent.

"No, no," Mary said. "The fresh air's good for the little ones."

Several people were on the street and many spoke to Magnolia, telling her how much they missed her cooking now that she wasn't working at the Dodge House anymore. As they were passing the laundry, a young woman came out carrying a canvas bag.

"Oh, what cute little girls," she said as she set her heavy load down. "Are they twins?"

Magnolia had seen the young woman before. She knew she stayed at the Red House, but because she often saw her in the morning, she didn't think she was one of the prostitutes.

"No, they're just sisters," Magnolia said. "I've seen you before. Do you work at the Red . . . I mean the Devil's Den?" Even after all this time, Magnolia had a hard time thinking of the Red House by any other name.

The girl's face flushed as she looked down, not wanting to make eye contact with Magnolia.

"I clean the rooms and do the laundry."

"And what's your name?"

"I'm Cetti. Cetti Marcelli."

"Well, Cetti Marcelli, I'm glad to meet you. If you'd ever want to get another job sometime, I know that the Dodge House needs someone to do the same thing you're doing now except that . . ."

"Oh, Mrs. Willis, I couldn't leave my sister. She works at the Devil's Den and she needs me."

"I'm sure she does," Magnolia said, curious as to how this girl knew her name. "I'd like it very much if you'd call me Magnolia."

"Magnolia." The girl laughed. "Did anyone ever call you Maggie?"

"As a matter of fact, there were some people who called me Maggie, but that was a long time ago."

"I asked because my real name is Concetta, but nobody knows that."

"Well, now I do. Thank you for sharing it."

"Miss Magnolia, you're different from most of the other women who live here, at least those who don't..."

"Cetti! You little whore!" a man's voice shouted. "Get back over here!"

The rude man was Luke Slater; he was charging across the street with long strides.

"Oh!" Cetti said, and Magnolia saw the frightened look on her face. "I've got to go." She picked up her laundry bag and started to leave.

"Wait." Magnolia said very quietly. "Is that man mean to you? Does he ever beat you?"

"No!" Cetti replied, though the way she answered the question gave lie to the response.

Instantly, Magnolia was transported back in time to New Orleans and the Lafitte's Blacksmith Shop Bar where she and Arabella had worked together, or before that *Le Plaisir d'un Gentleman.* Both were brothels, and she had felt the sting of the whip on more than one occasion.

"You know, you don't have to stay over there."

"I could never leave my sister, I'm afraid they would…"

"You leave my whores alone," Slater demanded. "You don't own the saloon anymore."

"It wasn't her fault, Mr. Slater," Cetti said. "I was just talking to the little girls."

Slater grabbed Cetti and began pulling her across the street.

"Let her go," Magnolia yelled, as she tried to keep him from taking her. "She's just a child."

Slater stopped as he slacked his pull on Cetti, instead grabbing Magnolia by the hair. "Do you want to take her place? I'll bet you do. We all seen your man drive out of town."

Magnolia slapped Luke Slater, doing so before she even gave it a second thought.

Slater glared at her, then the glare turned into an evil grin. "Well now, Missy, you're a feisty one. But that's what it's like when a woman's got a touch of the tar-brush."

"Get out of my sight," Magnolia ordered.

"Oh, I'm doin' just that," Slater replied. He reached out and grabbed Cetti's arm. "And I'll be takin' this little whore with me."

He jerked Cetti so hard that she called out in pain.

"Shut up," Slater yelled, as he backhanded the girl. "Shut up, or I'll give you somethin' to cry about."

As Magnolia watched Slater drag Cetti across the street, she formed her hands into fists, seething inside, as she was helpless to do anything about it.

Chapter Twenty-One

PRIVATE AL LEMON had the reputation of being the worst soldier at Fort Dodge, though Sergeant Caviness, the stable NCO, said that he believed he could make the claim that Lemon was the worst soldier in the entire United States army. But just because he was not a good soldier didn't mean he wasn't a smart man. Lemon happened upon a situation that he knew he could exploit, if he would just play his cards right.

He shared his idea with Lum Fargo, a man he had known at Fort Leavenworth. Fargo had been dishonorably discharged from the army, and now worked for the Slaters at the Devil's Den.

"Lemon has offered to make a deal with us," Fargo told Mack Slater after the introduction was made.

"What kind of deal?"

"I can get you some horses, at least ten of 'em, and it'll only cost ya ten dollars apiece," Lemon said.

"Ten dollars? Where're you goin' to get horses for ten dollars apiece?"

"It'll be easy," Fargo said. "Lemon'll be with a detail of soldiers that's goin' to be takin' ten remounts to Camp Supply."

"But how big's this detail gonna be?" Mack asked.

"Just me and three others," Lemon said.

"And when will it head out?"

"We'll be leavin' tomorrow mornin' fore the sun comes up."

Mack nodded. "All right, I can give you ten dollars apiece."

A big smile crossed Lemon's face as he held out his hand.

"What's that for?" Fargo asked.

"My money," Lemon said.

Mack and Fargo both laughed. "That ain't how it works, son. You get your money when we get the horses."

***

The blackboard had been Jeter's idea and it had been mounted on the back wall of the freight office. On the blackboard was a list of the wagon drivers, where they were going, and what they were carrying. While Cade was out tending to the mules, and Jacob was looking over the spare parts needed to keep the wagons in repair, Jeter was in the office writing on the blackboard.

Drivers	_Load_
Destination	
Pullen/Cahill	_Tinware_
Iuka	
Foster/Matthews	_Stoves_
Caldwell	
McKnight/Keaton	_Saddles and_
tack Camp Supply	
Morris/Lambdin	_Groceries_
Cheyenne Agency	

"What do you think of it?" Jeter asked, pointing to the board.

"Looks like a pretty good idea to me," Cade answered. "Have Morris and Lambdin left yet?"

"No, they're still down at the depot loading up. John Miles sent a telegram from the agency saying they're about plum out of flour," Jeter said. "We're sending 'em 126 hundred-pound bags. Do you think that'll be enough?"

"It's a lot of flour," Cade said as he began opening a drawer. "Where's that . . . ?" He was interrupted when a woman stuck her head in the door.

"Hello?" she said, tentatively.

"Good morning, Mrs. Lambdin."

"Ah, Mr. McCall. Have Dan and Walt left yet?"

"No, they're still here, at least they're still in town. Do you need something?"

"It's nothing," Rowena replied with a smile. She held up a sack. "I fried a chicken for them this morning. Dan loves fried chicken, and he said Walt did too." She laughed. "He didn't come right out and ask for it, you understand. He just said that he and Walt really 'liked' it."

"Well, it looks like his hinting about it got the job done, didn't it?" Cade said, with a little chuckle.

"Yes, it did. I made enough for both of them," Mrs. Lambdin said. "Shall I leave it here for them?"

"They're at the depot, and it looks like they'll be there for a while. Why don't you take it on down to them?" Cade said. "I'm sure they will appreciate it."

"I'll just do that. You have a good day, now."

The next day, Sergeant Gulliver and his detail made camp on Sand Creek. He and the three privates who were with him were sitting around a campfire. The coffee was already made, and several slices of bacon were twitching in the pan. There were fourteen horses tethered to a rope that stretched between two trees, the ten remounts for Camp Supply, and the horses the soldiers were riding.

"Spivey, is it true that you fell in love with one o' them whores in town?" Private Whitman asked. "'Cause if it's true, which one of 'em is it? The reason I ask is 'cause they's one of 'em that's in love with me."

"Which one's in love with you?" Private Spivey asked.

"Why whichever one I give the two dollars to," Whitman replied, and the others laughed.

"I knew a whore back in Jefferson Barracks," Sergeant Gulliver said. "Then when I seen her again at Fort Leavenworth, she was married to a captain." Gulliver chuckled. "That captain give me ten dollars a month not to tell nobody. Yes, sir, I had a sweet deal while I was stationed there, but then one day I got orders to come to Fort Dodge. 'N I know damn well it was the captain what got me shipped out."

One of the horses whinnied, and it was answered by another. Several of them began moving around, tossing their heads and stamping their feet.

"Sarge, them horses is gettin' spooked over somethin'," Spivey said.

"Yeah, they do seem a bit antsy, don't they?

Private Lemon got up and moved away from the fire.

"Where you goin' Lemon?" Sergeant Gulliver asked.

"I gotta take a piss. You don't want me pissin' close to where the bacon is cookin' do you?"

"Sarge, you want me to take a look at them horses?" Whitman asked.

"Yeah, I don't reckon it'd hurt to take a look around," Gulliver said. "Could be nothin' more 'n a fox or somethin' or maybe…"

That was as far as Sergeant Gulliver got before Weasel Slater, Dutch Henry Kraus, Lum Fargo, and Silas Carter came riding into the soldiers' camp, with their guns blazing. It was over within seconds; Gulliver, Whitman, and Spivey going down without ever even drawing their weapons.

"Looks like there's more'n ten horses here," Weasel said.

"Yeah, the extras is what we was a ridin'" Lemon said. "Looks like you boys can count them as a bonus."

"That's mighty thoughtful of you," Weasel said "This worked out right easy. You done real good." Weasel took out a hundred dollars and gave it to Lemon. "Do you think maybe we can do business again?"

"What kind of business?" Lemon asked.

"Well, just kinda keep your ear to the ground. If you hear of somethin' else that's gonna happen, like any more horses that's bein' took somewhere without too many goin' with 'em, then we can steal 'em."

"I can do that," Lemon said, as he shoved the money down in his pocket.

"Good." Then suddenly and unexpectedly, Weasel shot Lemon, hitting him in the arm.

"What the hell did you do that for?" Lemon shouted in anger. "I done what I told you I was goin' to do."

"You want the army to think that you was the one told us about them horses?" Weasel asked.

"Hell no, but why'd you have to shoot me?"

"It's just a little ole scratch," Weasel said, "and it'll show the army that you put up a fight to save the horses, but you was the only one that survived."

Lemon stared at Weasel for a long moment, holding his hand over the wound in his upper arm.

"The bullet went clean through, didn't it?" Dutch Henry asked.

"Yeah," Lemon said.

"Well then, all you got to do is put a bandage around it to stop the bleedin' 'n you'll be all right." Weasel chuckled. "Hell, you'll be more 'n all right, you'll be a hero."

Lemon smiled. "Yeah," he said. "Yeah, I will be a hero, won't I?"

"A hero with a hunnert dollars in your pocket," Weasel said.

Cade was in the Alhambra Saloon that evening, having his dinner. He was having one beer with his dinner, a self-imposed limit since he had emerged from the year-long drunken bout with depression.

"You son of a bitch!" Someone shouted. The words were hurled in anger, the same kind of anger that preceded gunfire and Cade, as did everyone else in the saloon, braced himself for the shooting that was sure to come.

But there was no shooting. Instead Cade looked up to see Bat Masterson holding a gun on a very angry man.

"I think perhaps you should leave, now," Bat said to the man, making a motion toward the door with his pistol.

The man glared at Bat, then got up and left the table where he, Bat, and two others had been playing poker.

"Gentlemen, I've lost my desire to play," Bat said to the two others. Seeing Cade he came toward him.

"Mind if I join you?"

"Sit down. What was that all about?"

"That uncouth lout accused me of cheating, and if that wasn't enough in itself, he also drew a gun on me. Or at least, he attempted to. As you can see, I was faster." He patted the gun butt, which was back in the holster.

"Would you have killed him?"

"I didn't have to."

"That doesn't answer my question. Would you have killed him?"

"Well, I . . . I don't know, I . . ."

"It's too late, you're dead," Cade said.

"What do you mean?"

"Bat, it isn't how fast you are. It's how willing you are to follow through. Most efficient gunmen are nowhere near as fast as you are. But they have something you lack. They have the willingness to kill their adversary. And until you develop that same . . . willingness, you are a sheep among wolves."

Suddenly, and shockingly, Cade drew his pistol.

"You little son of a bitch I'll . . ." that was as far as the man got before Cade shot him down. It was the same man with whom Bat had had the earlier altercation. Only this time, there was a gun in the man's hands.

"You just saved my life," Bat said.

"No, I just gave you an extension. And if you aren't ready to kill someone anytime you're forced to draw your gun, it won't be a very long extension."

"Five hundred flint buffalo skins," Stone Eagle said. Stone Eagle was chief of the Kiowa village where Weasel had brought the horses they had stolen from the army.

"Buffalo skins? Ain't you got no white man's money?" Weasel asked.

"Take 'em, Weasel," Dutch Henry said.

"What? What do we want with five hunnert buffalo skins?" Weasel asked. "What are we goin' to do with 'em out here in the middle of nowhere?"

"We'll take 'em back to Dodge City?" Dutch Henry said. "We can get three dollars apiece."

"Three dollars? That don't make no sense. We paid ten dollars apiece for them horses."

"Damn, Weasel or you as dumb as you look? Three dollars a skin," Dutch Henry explained patiently. "Five hunnert skins means fifteen hunnert dollars."

Weasel finally understood what Dutch Henry was talking about, and the frown on Weasel's face turned to a smile. "Yeah!" he said. "Yeah, let's do it!"

"Only one problem," Lum Fargo said. "How we goin' to get 'em to Dodge?"

"We'll get us a wagon 'n a team," Weasel said.

"And how much will that cost us?" Fargo asked.

Weasel smiled. "It won't cost nothin'. We'll just wait is all."

That same afternoon, Weasel was looking down at Sully Road when he saw what he waiting for—a large freight wagon being pulled by four mules. He could hear the squeak and rattle of the wagon, the hoof beats of the four mules, as well as the conversation of the two men who were on the wagon.

Weasel smiled. He'd show Luke and Mack. He could pull this off just fine without their help.

Ten minutes later, the wagon started back toward Stone Eagle's village, with the two drivers lying dead on the road behind them. Their bodies were already drawing a circle of vultures.

When they reached Stone Eagle's village, several of the Indians gathered around the wagon.

"Look," Dutch Henry said. "We've brought you a gift." He pointed to the canvas that covered the load.

"Gift?" Stone Eagle asked.

"Yes, a gift for our friends."

"That is good," Stone Eagle said, as he motioned for the women to come. When they looked under the covering, they all began talking at once, angry scowls on their faces.

"What's wrong with 'em? Don't they like our presents?"

"They want cloth, they want beads, they want umbrella. Not this," Stone Eagle said as he threw back the canvas.

"Well, you're going to have to take it, 'cause we sure as hell can't haul it and the buffalo robes."

Stone Eagle spoke sharply to the women, and they began unloading the wagon.

"Have we heard word from Morris and Lamdin?" Cade asked, coming into the office.

"Nope. They should have reached the Agency yesterday, but we haven't heard from Miles," Jeter said.

"It's too bad Darlington died. He always sent a telegram back to us telling us the wagon got there, or if it was late he would send somebody out to look for it," Jacob said.

"It could be they're broken down somewhere," Cade said. "It was going to the Indians anyway, so they aren't likely to cause any trouble. And no highwayman's going to steal a load of flour."

"You're probably right. But it just seems to me like we should have heard by now."

"I tell you what, if we haven't heard anything by tomorrow, I'll go look for them," Cade said.

"You mean we'll go look for them," Jeter said.

"No, I'll go by myself. Or maybe I'll take Bat with me. He needs to get out of town for a while."

Chapter Twenty-Two

DUTCH HENRY was driving the wagon, and his horse was tied on to the back while Weasel, Fargo, and Carter were riding just ahead.

"Hey, Weasel," Dutch Henry called.

Weasel turned his horse to come back to the wagon. "What do you want?"

"I been thinkin', we can't take these hides to Dodge City."

"And why not? That's the best place to sell the hides."

"Look at the sign that's wrote on the side of the wagon. This here wagon's from Dodge," Dutch Henry said. "If we go prancin' into town you know somebody's gonna see us."

"Hell, Weasel, one wagon looks purt near like another 'n, don't it?" Carter asked. "More 'n likely, there won't no one that'll even pay any attention that sign no how. I don't see no problem."

"Well, there is a problem," Weasel said. "This wagon belongs to Cade McCall. 'N he could be trouble."

"So, what are we goin' to do?" Fargo asked. "If we don't sell these here skins, we just lost our money."

"I don't know yet. Let me think about it."

As the four men progressed toward Dodge City, they stopped at Bluff Creek to allow the mules and horses to drink.

"You two wait here for a while," Weasel said. "I'm goin' to scout ahead, some."

"You think they'll have the law out lookin' for this wagon?" Weasel asked.

"There more'n likely ain't been time for the wagon to get back, so there prob'ly ain't nobody missed it yet. But if someone found the bodies, 'n knowed who they are, they could be out looking for the wagon. At any rate, it don't hurt none to be careful."

Leaving his three cohorts behind, Weasel went ahead for about another mile. That was when he saw the farm. More importantly, he saw the farm wagon, and with a triumphant smile on his face, he hurried back to the others.

"Come on," he said. "I think I just found us another wagon."

Red Jenkins was pumping water when he saw the wagon approaching with three outriders.

"Ma!" he called. "Better make up a pone of cornbread to go with them ham 'n beans. Looks like we're goin' to have company."

Setting the bucket of water down, he walked out to greet the visitors.

"Welcome, boys," he said. "I hope you'll be wantin' to break bread with us. It gets awful lonely here, so far from anyone else."

"You've got no neighbors?" one of the riders asked, as he dismounted.

"None within twenty miles. The name's Jenkins. Edna, that's my wife, why she just put in a pone of cornbread."

"Cornbread? Well, that sounds like it'll be real tasty. The name's Slater." Weasel extended his hand. "These here boys work for me."

"Don't know as if I've heard that name in these parts," Jenkins said. "What is it you're a' carryin' under that there canvas? Looks awful loaded down."

"Buffalo skins," Weasel said. "We work for an outfit outta Dodge City. We're takin' the skins up to him."

"Oh, yes, I see the sign on the side of the wagon. You boys must be new. I've met most of the Harrison, McCall, and Willis drivers, 'n don't recall ever seein' any of you before."

"That's right, we're new."

"That's a heavy load you got there, it'll take you two, maybe three more days to get there."

"I expect it will, but that's what we get paid for," Weasel said.

"Red, don't keep them gentlemen standin' outside all day," Edna called. "Bring 'em on into the house!"

Both Red and Edna were in their sixties, and both showed the results of a lifetime of hard work. Edna had been a brunette at one time, but now her hair was literally laced with gray. Her face was wrinkled, and a tiredness showed in her eyes.

Red showed the effects of his age even more than Edna. His hair was not only gray, it was thinning. He had a full, unkempt beard.

"What do you grow here, on the farm?" Dutch Henry asked later, as the six of them sat around a table that was filled with food.

"Corn, mostly, though some alfalfa too. 'Course we keep a garden for ourselves, but next week or so, there'll be some soldier boys from Ft. Larned that'll be comin' down for the hay, then after they get the hay, why, me 'n Edna will be takin' us a load of corn on up to Wichita."

"I saw the wagon. You'll be usin' that to take your corn?"

"Yes, sir, 'n a good sturdy wagon she is, too. Why we made over a thousand bushels of corn last year, 'n hauled it all up to Wichita. Nary a problem." Jenkins laughed. "We had a fine time in Wichita too, didn't we, Edna?"

"I'll say we did," Edna said. "We et at one o' them . . . restaurants, they call them . . . a restaurant is a different from a café. They're a bit more fancy."

"Well now, Mrs. Jenkins, I don't believe you could possibly have a better meal in one o' them restaurants than this here meal you're 'a feedin' us," Dutch Henry said.

"I agree, Carter added. "This here is the best meal I've had in a coon's age. I can see why you married her, Mr. Jenkins. Why, she's not only a handsome woman, she can cook too."

"Oh, how you men carry on," Edna said, blushing slightly and turning her head in embarrassment.

"We been married some forty-seven years now ain't it Edna? I was twenty, 'n the missus, why, she weren't quite sixteen."

"We had to sneak out in the middle of the night to do it," Edna said. She reached over to take her husband's hand. "Papa didn't much want me to marry this here'n, but I knowed soon as I seen 'im, that Red was the man for me."

Red and Edna looked at each other and had their guests been more discerning, they would have been able to see the love in the eyes of this old married couple.

But Weasel and the others were totally insensitive to such things.

"Say, Mr. Jenkins, I wonder if you'd mind me lookin' over your wagon?" Weasel asked as they were finishing their meal."

Red broke the eye contact he had with his wife. "You want to see my wagon? Well, sure, of course you can look at it. Don't know why you're so interested, though."

"Well, as I told you, we're kind of new in the freightin' business," Weasel said. "So I'm always interested in wagons 'n such."

"All right, come on, then. I'll be glad to show it to you."

As Weasel and the others followed Red Jenkins outside, Edna began cleaning up after the meal as she hummed a nonsensical tune. In this isolated country, company was always welcome.

Dutch Henry pushed on the side of the wagon while Weasel checked each wheel. Fargo examined the tongue and double-tree.

Jenkins laughed. "The way you boys is a lookin' this wagon over, you'd think you're 'a wantin' to buy it."

"We're takin' it," Weasel said.

"What? What do you mean, you're takin' it? I ain't a' sellin'."

"And we ain't buyin'," Weasel said, shooting him.

"Red?" Edna called from the house. "Red, what was that shot?"

"Mrs. Jenkin's maybe you'd better come out here quick," Weasel called. "There's been a terrible accident."

"What?" Edna shouted. "Red? Red!" Edna hurried from the house to the wagon, where she saw her husband lying on the ground. "My God! What happened?"

"I killed him," Weasel said in a calm, and conversational voice.

"You what?" Edna turned to look at Weasel, who was pointing his pistol at her.

"I said I killed him," Weasel repeated, as he pulled the trigger.

Edna fell close to Red, and with her dying breath, reached out to clutch Red's hand in her's.

"Now, ain't that sweet?" Weasel said, his voice totally devoid of emotion. "Come on, let's get these skins transferred to the other wagon."

As the men began moving the skins from one wagon to the other, a hound dog came loping up to the bodies, sniffed both of them, then lay down near them and with his head on his paws, began to whine.

After about half an hour the new wagon was loaded, and the mules hitched to it.

"What are we goin' to do with this wagon?" Fargo asked, pointing to the freight wagon.

"Burn it," Dutch Henry said.

"Good idea," Weasel replied. "We'll burn the wagon, and the house."

"The house? Why are we goin' to burn the house?" Carter asked.

"So nobody finds these two. We'll burn the wagon, the house and the bodies."

When they started to move Edna's body, the dog bared its teeth and began to grow at them.

"This damn dog won't let us touch the old woman," Carter said.

Dutch Henry pulled his pistol and shot the dog in the head. The dog died instantly.

"What'd you do that for? He was just a dog."

"He wanted to be with 'em, now he is," Dutch Henry said. "Come on, let's get this fire goin'."

A short while later, with the wagon and the house in flames behind them, Weasel and the others got under way.

***

"This wasn't done by Indians," Cade said, as he and Bat stared down at the bodies of Morris and Lamdin. The birds had had four days to work on them, but still the bodies had not been mutilated the way an Indian would do it.

"Why would anyone do this?" Cade asked. "Who can be this evil?" "Maybe they just wanted the cargo," Bat suggested. "The team and wagon are gone."

"One hundred twenty-six bags of flour? Who kills two men for that?"

"There is, of course, one other possibility," Bat said. "It's quite likely we are dealing with a person or persons who need no motives at all, save the very worst. We might well be dealing directly with evil incarnate."

"Bat, quit your psychologizing for once," Cade said as he began finding a spot to bury the men.

"I'm not looking forward to this," Cade said. "I can still see her bringing fried chicken to Dan and Walt."

"Do you want me to come, too?" Jeter asked.

"You don't have to," Cade said. "I can do it by myself."

"I know, but I want to come. Especially for Lambdin's kids. Maybe I can help."

"I guess you do have a better perspective on this than I do. How old were you when your ma and pa were killed?"

"I was five," Jeter said. "I'll never forget when I crawled out from under the floor of that old house. It's a good thing Indians didn't burn the place down, or I wouldn't be here."

"I know that was bad, but look at the good side. Your own mother couldn't love you anymore than Mary Hatley loves you."

Jeter looked directly at Cade. "You mean like a man could love a daughter that wasn't his own flesh and blood?"

"Yes, like a man could love a daughter," Cade said and then he continued. "I know you won't believe this, but I think I'll start looking for a wife."

"It won't work if you're going to find a woman just to be Chantal's mother," Jeter said. "You've got to find someone you can love as much as you loved Arabella."

"It'll never happen."

"That's what you're saying now, but that'll change if you just let it."

Cade hit Jeter on the shoulder. "Tell me, have you been learning all this stuff from Masterson?"

"I don't know what you're talking about."

"Bat. He's the amateur psychologist around here."

Chapter Twenty-Three

DAN LAMBDIN lived in a sod house just west of town. He had two very young children who were playing out front when Cade and Jeter arrived.

"Well, Mr. McCall, Mr. Willis," Rowena Lambdin greeted them with a broad smile. Have you word on Dan? I expected him back yesterday. Did the wagon break down?"

"Mrs. Lambdin . . ." Cade started, then he stopped, searching for the words he could use to tell her.

The smile left her face. "It's Dan, isn't it?"

"What?"

"You have come to tell me about Dan. Something has happened to him, hasn't it? Has he…is he…?

Cade looked down, still unable to answer.

Rowena raised her fist to her mouth and bit on her knuckle for a moment before she spoke again.

"I knew it," she said, when she was able to form the words. "I don't know how I knew, but I knew."

Although there was palpable grief in her voice, Rowena didn't break down, and Cade was thankful for that.

"Mrs. Lambdin . . . Rowena, if there is anything we can do for you, please let us know."

"Where is he? I would like to see him."

"No, you wouldn't have wanted to see him, trust me."

"Wouldn't have wanted? You mean it's too late?"

"We buried both of them out on the trail."

Rowena hung her head, then, after a pause she spoke again. "Yes, that is best. Dan loved driving, he loved being out on the road. That's a fitting place for him to be."

"What will you do now?" Jeter asked.

"Dan was trying to save enough money for us to move back to St. Louis," Rowena said. "Both of our families are there."

"Would you like to go there?"

"Yes, I think I would."

"We'll buy the train tickets for you and the children," Jeter offered.

"Thank you, I would appreciate that."

"If you would like, I'll sent my mother over to help you get ready to go. She's very good with children."

"The children," Rowena said. "I'm going to have to tell them, but they're so young, I'm not sure they'll understand."

"Children are stronger than most people give them credit for," Jeter said. "They'll come through this all right. Trust me, I know."

Cade and Jeter were having a drink at the Dodge House having just come from the train station.

"That was a good thing you did, paying for Mrs. Lambdin and her kids to go back to Saint Louis," Jeter said.

"She couldn't have stayed here without a husband. She isn't strong like Arabella was, and Magnolia is. Look at that Markley woman that Jacob was trying to hitch up with. How long did it take before she was back on the train to Ohio?"

"There's going to be somebody out there for you, if you can ever stop measuring every woman against Arabella."

"I know, but she was one of a kind. It might take a while."

Weasel Slater looked around as he and the other three with him had just arrived in Dodge City. He pulled his hat down to shield his face, even though his full beard gave him what he thought would be a disguise.

"Who's this here guy that's gonna take these hides off us," Fargo asked.

"His name's Lobenstein, and he's got a place down by the depot," Weasel said.

"What about sellin' 'em here?" Carter said as they passed by Charles Rath and Company. "Just look at all them hides theys got piled up in that lot. Why don't we just sell 'em here."

"Because Charles Rath knows who I am, and Lobenstein don't," Weasel said.

"That I understand," Carter said.

When they reached the depot, Weasel sent Fargo in to talk with Lobenstein. It was only a minute before he returned to the wagon.

"Your man ain't here. They say if we want to get rid of this load, we have to deal with Rath."

Weasel let out a sigh. "Hell, nothin's going right. All this because the damn Indians don't use white man's money."

They had to go around the block to get the wagon turned, and when they stopped in front of Rath's store, Alonzo Webster came out to the wagon with a ledger in his hand.

"How many you selling, gents?" Alonzo asked.

"Five hundred good clean skins," Weasel said.

Alonzo jerked his head around. "Well I'll be damned, if it ain't Weasel Slater. You know the army's still lookin' for you?"

"You mean for killin' that feller that come after me with a axe? That's all been took care of," Weasel lied. "Even the army knows that it was self-defense now."

"I hope that's so," Charles Rath said as he stepped out of his store. "I wouldn't like to see our town closed down again."

"No, sir, that ain't goin' to happen no more," Weasel assured him.

"So you have five hundred skins," Rath said. "Let me take a look at them."

Alonzo pulled the canvas back and Rath examined a few of the skins.

"Good skins," Rath said nodding his head. "Looks like they were cleaned by Indians."

"Yeah, we bought 'em from the Injuns."

"I'll give you two dollars apiece for them," Wright said.

"Two dollars? I thought they was goin' for three dollars?"

"Three dollars from Lobenstein, but he's not here right now. And who knows what the market will be when he gets back. Two dollars is all I'm prepared to pay right now."

"All right," Weasel said, reluctantly. "I know I could get more if I wait till he gets back, but I need to get 'em off my hands. How soon will I get the money?"

"As soon as we get 'em counted," Rath said. "Alonzo, go round up the boys and let's get these on the pile."

A few minutes later, half-a-dozen men were gathered around the wagon, unloading the skins. One of the men stopped, and looked at the mules.

"Hey, where'd you get these mules?" he asked.

"Why are you asking, Sam?" Rath asked.

"I know these mules," he said. "I seen 'em when I was workin' for Mr. Young. This here mule's Rhoda, that one's Harry, that one's Bridget, 'n that one's Cooter. They was Mr. Young's, but now they belong to Harrison and McCall."

"Are you sure?" Rath asked.

"Damn right I'm sure. I've put them same mules in harness . . . wait a minute, these here is the same mules that Lambdin 'n Morris was a drivin' on that last trip."

Wright looked at Weasel. "Sam's asked a good question, Mr. Slater. Where did you get these mules?"

"From the same place we got the skins," Weasel answered, quickly. "The Injuns sold this here wagon 'n these mules to us so's we'd have a way to bring these skins up here."

"That's it then," Sam said. "We've been wonderin' who it was that kilt Lamdin 'n Morris, 'n now we know. It was the Injuns."

"They may have wound up with the mules," Rath said. "But I don't think they killed the drivers. Both Cade and Bat said their bodies weren't mutilated the way an Indian would do it."

"Wait a minute," Weasel said. "Are you a' tellin' me that the fellers that was drivin' these mules was kilt?"

"Yes."

"By damn, if I had knowd that, I wouldn't have never bought these here mules."

Sam took a closer look at the wagon. "This here wagon don't belong to Harrison though."

"How do you know that?" Rath asked. "You know they are missing a wagon."

"They only got four wagons, 'n their mark's on all of 'em, 'n there ain't no mark on this'n."

"Well then, if these mules belong to Harrison why I reckon he'd be right happy to get 'em back," Weasel said.

"He probably would," Rath said.

"You reckon he'd be happy enough to give us a reward?"

"Well, I don't have an answer for that question."

A few minutes later with Dutch Henry, Fargo, and Carter paid off, Weasel took the mules and the wagon down to Harrison, McCall, and Willis.

"I was told that these here was your mules," Weasel said.

Jacob and Cade examined the mules.

"This is Rhoda, look at her ear," Jacob said.

"And this is Harry," Cade said. Cade looked toward Weasel. "These are our mules, all right. May I ask how you came by them?"

"It's like I told Charles Rath, I bought 'em from some Injuns," Weasel said. "But I didn' have no idea they was stolen."

"How much did you pay for them?"

"Fifty dollars apiece. That should 'a give me an idea somethin' was wrong, 'cause I'm sure they're worth a lot more than that."

"They're worth at least two hundred dollars apiece," Jacob said. "But I'll be glad to give you your money back."

"Maybe with a little extra, for a reward?" Weasel suggested. "After all, I brung 'em here from down in the Territory."

"Technically, Mr. Slater, I don't have to give you anything. You're in possession of stolen property. If I were you, I'd take the money and be happy with it."

"What about the wagon? Since your wagon was burnt up 'n all, maybe you'd like to buy this wagon from me."

Both Cade and Jacob looked up sharply.

"What do you mean our wagon was burned?" Cade asked.

"Well, I mean, ain't that what happened to it? Leastwise, that's what I heard happened to it. Are you saying it warn't burned?"

"We're saying nothing of the sort," Jacob said. "We don't know what happened to it."

"Yeah, well, I don't neither. I was just kind 'a speculatin' on account of what I heard, is all. I'll take the money for the mules and thank you for it."

Jacob gave Weasel two hundred dollars, then stood in the door watching as he walked away.

"Have you heard anywhere that our wagon was burned?" Jacob asked.

"No," Cade replied.

"Wouldn't you think that if that rumor was going around that we, being the owners of the wagon, would have heard it?"

"You'd think so."

"They said they bought the mules from the Indians, but I'm positive that Dan and Walt were not killed by Indians."

"Do you think the Slaters did it?" Jacob asked.

"I don't know. It's possible I guess, but if they were the ones who did it, why would they be stupid enough to bring the mules back to us?" Cade asked. "Besides, what's the reason? Dan and Walt were hauling flour."

"They don't need a reason," Jeter said, speaking for the first time. "Depravity is their middle name."

A week later an article of interest to Dutch Henry appeared in the *Dodge City Messenger*.

Farm Couple Die in Fire

> *A detachment of soldiers from Fort Larned called upon Mr. Al Jenkins of Comanche County for the purposes of purchasing alfalfa hay on Monday previous. This was in keeping with a*

contract that existed between Mr. Jenkins and the army.

To the shock of Sergeant Ernest Martell, the one in charge of the soldier detail, they discovered that the house had been totally destroyed by fire. Inside the house they found the charred bodies of Mr. and Mrs. Jenkins, as well their dog.

It is a mystery as to why the Jenkins and their dog were unable to exit the house, once the fire began. Sergeant Martell ordered his soldiers to bury the Jenkins on their farm. Their faithful dog lies beside them.

Dutch Henry found Weasel and read the article to him.

"Ha!" Weasel said, with a grin crossing his face. "I told you burnin' 'em was a good idea. We ain't gonna be havin' no more trouble out'a that job, and we's a lot richer than we would'a been if we'd just sold the horses."

Dodge City continued to grow in spite of the dwindling buffalo herd. According to the records for the Atchison, Topeka and Santa Fe Railroad, there were 497,163 hides shipped out in 1872 alone. As the winter wore on, more and more hunters were moving into the "no-man's land". This was a strip of land that separated Kansas from Texas and it was supposedly reserved for the several Indian tribes that had agreed to go onto reservations in exchange for the right to hunt buffalo.

Even though the hunters drifted farther and farther south, they always returned to Dodge City to sell their robes. Dodge was still a wide-open town, with more and more saloons—now twenty-six in number. And still no law existed except for one US Marshal who was technically located in Hays City. On his rare visits to Dodge City, his attempt to corral the rowdies was met with taunts and ridicule.

It was in this climate that the most successful business in town remained the Devil's Den Saloon. It was now open twenty-four hours a day, and the noise coming from the establishment was as loud at two o'clock in the morning as it was at two o'clock in the afternoon. In addition to the noise of shouts, screams, laugher, and off-key music there was, too often, the sound of gunfire.

One day in early spring of 1873, a big man with a dark, swooping moustache and narrow brown eyes rode into town. A knife fight had carved away part of his upper lip, leaving him permanently scarred. That same fight had left his opponent permanently dead.

Dismounting in front of the Devil's Den, the man, who went by the name of Edge Dunn, tied off his horse and went inside, moving away from the door to put his back to the wall as he perused the patrons of the busy saloon. He saw the man he was looking for at the back of the saloon, playing the wheel of fortune. He seemed to be winning, and one of the saloon girls was standing beside him, cheering him on. Dunn walked up to the man.

"I've been looking for you, Brock," Dunn said.

There was an implied challenge in the tone that brought all activity to a halt. Even the man who was about to spin the wheel froze.

The man called Brock turned away from the wheel, shoved the girl aside, and smiled, though there was no humor in his smile.

"It looks like you found me."

In a saloon that was known for the high level of noise, there was now dead silence as, for a long moment, the two men stared at each other. Then, without a word of warning, Brock made a grab for his pistol, but Dunn beat him to the draw and within a heartbeat, Brock lay dead on the floor.

Clemmie, the girl who had been standing next to Brock, looked down at his body, then at Dunn, who was still holding the smoking gun in his hand.

"Mister," she said, "you just cost me two dollars. This man was about to go upstairs with me."

"You haven't lost anything," Dunn said, offering her his hand.

Clemmie flashed him a big smile. "All right," she said. "I haven't lost a thing." Stepping over Brock's body she hooked her arm through Dunn's and they headed for the stairway.

That very day Mack Slater hired Edge Dunn. He was to be a private security guard for the saloon. Nobody knew much about him, but everybody speculated.

"Why, he kilt twelve men down in Texas a' fore he come up here."

"It's fifteen men that he kilt, 'n it warn't in Texas, it was in Wyoming."

Edge Dunn sat in a chair on a raised platform that allowed him to see everything that was going on out on the floor. He had a double-barrel shotgun across his lap, a rifle by his side, and a holstered pistol. In most cases, a simple warning from Dunn was enough to deter anyone who might have a hostile thought. But that wasn't enough for everybody, and within a month after arriving in Dodge City, he had killed four more men. Every killing, according to witnesses, was justified.

Chapter Twenty-Four

JETER WAS posting trip information on the blackboard when Jolly Hartzog, a young man who worked for Robert Wright, came into the office.

"Mr. Willis?"

"Yes, Jolly, what do you need?"

"Mr. Wright has called a meetin' of the town directors 'n businessmen for two o'clock this afternoon."

"Two o'clock? All right, we'll be there."

"We?"

"Yes, Mr. McCall, Mr. Harrison, and I."

"I don't know if he wants them to come too. He sent me down to tell you, is all I know."

"You did say directors *and* businessmen didn't you?"

"Yes, sir, that's what he told me to say."

"Then Mr. McCall, Mr. Harrison, and I will be there."

"Yes, sir, I'll tell 'im."

At two o'clock that afternoon the Rath and Company store closed their doors to business. Cade, Jeter, and Jacob joined at least twenty other businessmen finding a place to sit or stand anywhere they could. Jeter noticed both Mack and Luke Slater were present as well, and he made his way to the opposite side of the room.

When all had gathered, Robert Wright stepped up front and called for quiet.

"Gentlemen," he began, "it has been since last August that several of us in this room drew up the papers to make Dodge City a town. While that process has been as slow as . . . well, as slow as molasses on ice, the lawlessness and the killings have gone on. According to Eb Collar, I believe we have had fifteen killings this winter alone."

"I can tell you how to stop that, and stop it right now," Winston Sweeny said. He pointed to the Slater brothers. "Ever body in this room knows that if that damn hell hole the Slaters run was shut down, why I'd say ninety percent of our trouble would stop. We all know trouble spills out of the Devil's Den and it spreads into all our places of business. And we can't stop it."

"I've been here since the beginning," Frederic Zimmerman said, "and from the beginning we've had our troubles."

"But it warn't like this," Sweeny said. "Does anybody remember when that place was the Red House? It was a damn fine place to go back then—no whores, no fights, and most of all no killings. I say kick the Slaters out."

"This is a meeting of the businessmen of this town, ain't it?" Mack retorted. "We're businessmen, so we have every right to be here."

"Mr. Slater is correct," Wright said. "He and his brother are businessmen and they have the right to be here."

"All right, then get back to the point of this meeting," George Cox said. "I need to get back to the Dodge House."

"We need to bring law and order to Dodge City."

Most in the room laughed.

"Tell us somethin' we don't know," Zimmerman said. "Ford County isn't even organized enough to have a county sheriff, so even if we was to appoint a marshal, he wouldn't have any authority."

"I was thinking more along the lines of a law enforcement committee," Wright said.

"What kind of committee?" Sweeny asked.

"Just a . . . committee that would take care of things," Wright said without being specific.

"Bob, you wouldn't be talking about vigilantes, would you?" Cade asked.

Wright paused for a moment before he replied. "All right, yes, maybe I am. The way I see it, a group of vigilantes, recognized by the community, is the only way we're going to be able to combat the lawlessness."

"The problem with vigilantes is they can too easily become their own law; then the cure would be as bad as the disease," Cade said.

"Then the way to overcome that possibility is to put only the best men on the vigilante committee," Charles Rath suggested.

"That depends on what you mean by the best men," Zimmerman said. "A lot of times the best men can't deal with the violence that this committee would have to confront."

"Fred's right. You have to fight fire with fire," Cox said.

"George, are you suggesting that we should engage some of the very people who are causing our problems?" Wright asked.

"I suppose I am. This way we could make their . . ." Cox stopped hunting for the right word. "I guess what I'm trying to say is that we can turn their meanness into a positive, rather than a negative thing."

"I'm afraid I have to agree with George and Fred," Charles Rath said.

"I have a suggestion," Mack Slater offered.

"What's your suggestion?" Wright asked.

"Edge Dunn. I think we should appoint him as the head of the vigilantes."

"Dunn? Absolutely not!" Herman Fringer said. "Why, he's been in Dodge less than a month, and he's already killed five men."

"And in every case the killing was justified," Slater replied.

"I don't know," Rath said. "Dunn's not a very likable person. We might have a hard time finding men who'd be willing to work with him."

"Let him recruit his own men," Slater suggested.

"What kind of a man would he find?" Zimmerman asked. "The men's Sunday school class, no doubt?" he added sarcastically.

"I don't think a Sunday school class would do it for you," Mack said. "You did say you wanted to fight fire with fire, didn't you? Well, that's exactly the kind of man

Dunn would round up. And believe me, a desperado would think twice a'fore he faced off agin' Edge."

"You know what, I hate to say it, but I think Slater's got a good idea," Sweeny said. "Ain't we tryin' to keep the outlaw out of our town? And who better to do it than someone who's not afraid to pull the trigger?"

"It could work," Rath agreed. "But I'd like to see Dunn work full time with the vigilantes."

"We couldn't expect him to do that unless we paid him," Zimmerman said. "And how would we do that? Let's face it. My hardware store doesn't need these vigilantes as much as all the saloons do."

"Don't have worry about that," Luke Slater said. "We been payin' Edge, and we'll keep on doin' it."

"That's all well and good, Slater," Cade said, "but wouldn't that mean Dunn would be working for you and not the town?"

"It don't matter," Slater replied, lifting his finger. "If the vigilantes do what we want 'em to, we'd all be better off. In the end, the outlaws would be took care of. Now ain't that what we want?"

"I say we take Slater's suggestion," Wright said. "I say we let Edge Dunn form up the vigilantes, and be the head of them."

"And I say we'll be opening a bag of worms if we do this," Jacob said.

"I agree," Fringer added.

"Why don't we put it to a vote?" Zimmerman suggested.

"All right," Wright said as he looked around the room. "The board of directors are all here. We can vote right now."

"No!" Mack Slater said quickly. "This here's the whole town's problem. I think everyone here should have a vote."

"I agree with Slater," George Cox said. "I'm not on the board of directors, but I damn sure am a business owner and I feel like I should have some say so in this."

"All right," Rath agreed. "I think the businessmen of the town should all have something to say about this. Mr. Chairman," he said, addressing Robert Wright, "I call the question."

Wright cleared his throat, then began to speak. "The question before the floor is, should the town of Dodge City hire Edge Dunn as a permanent member, and the chief of the Dodge City Vigilante Committee? And, should we let him recruit those who would serve as members of the committee?"

"Change the word 'hire' to 'appoint'," Cox said. "We can't afford to hire him, and Mack Slater already said he'd keep Dunn on the Devil's Den payroll."

Wright reposed the question, replacing the word hire with appoint. The motion carried, fourteen to nine. Cade, Jeter, and Jacob were part of the nine in opposition.

"I have a question," Jeter said, as everyone was congratulating themselves on taking the first steps. "Edge Dunn is being paid by the Slaters, but what about the vigilante members?"

"They'll be volunteers," Rath explained. "It'll be understood that they don't get paid."

"That's fine if the vigilantes are people who have a source of income, but we've just agreed to let Dunn do the recruiting. We don't know who he'll get so my question is how do they make a living?"

"That's a good point," Fringer said. "If Edge Dunn is choosing the members of the committee, how will they be making money?"

"We could charge a special tax," Slater suggested.

"No. No taxes," Wright said. "None of the citizens of the town would go along with it, and neither would I."

"I say we should cross that bridge when we come to it," Zimmerman said. "For now, the important thing is to get the committee organized."

"Hear, hear," one of the others responded.

As Cade, Jeter, and Jacob left the meeting, Cade shook his head. "I can't see anything good coming from this."

"Yeah," Jeter said. "Putting Edge Dunn in charge of keeping the peace is like . . ." he paused, searching for an analogy.

"Putting a fox in charge of the henhouse?" Jacob suggested.

"Yeah, putting a fox in charge of the henhouse."

"I suppose the only thing we can do is wait and see how it works out," Cade said.

From the Dodge City Messenger
COMMITTEE FORMED
  The Dodge City Town Company of Ford County held a meeting on the 4th instant, to which were invited, in addition to the members of the Board of Directors,

those gentlemen of the town who own and operate businesses.

The purpose of the meeting was to discuss what could be done about the increasing amount of murder, mayhem, and all other acts of violence taking place within the city limits. It was decided by all present that a law enforcement committee be formed to provide for the peace and tranquility of our new and growing community. Although this law enforcement committee lacks the jurisdiction of state law, or even country statutes, it does have the moral authority of a beleaguered body of citizens who are determined to rid their city of the despotism of desperadoes.

Edge Dunn, who is currently employed by the Devil's Den Saloon, has been appointed chief of the committee, and charged with the responsibility of recruiting its members.

ADVERTISEMENT
DODGE CITY TOWN COMPANY, FORD COUNTY, KANSAS. Inducements offered to actual settlers! Prospects of the town better than any other in the upper Arkansas Valley! Free Bridge across the Arkansas River! The town is a little over one year old, and contains over seventy buildings! Good school, hotel, etc. AT & SF RR depot in town... Enquire of: R. M.

Wright at Chas. Rath & Co. store or E. B. Kirk, Secy and Treasurer Advertisement.

Chapter Twenty-Five

FOR THE NEXT several days the citizens of the town were aware of new arrivals. The new men weren't buffalo hunters, nor were they storekeepers or lawyers or even gamblers. There was a sameness though: the look in their eyes, the confident, almost arrogant way they held themselves, the way they were dressed. But what was most noticeable about them was the way they wore their guns, with the holsters low, and kicked out for quick draw.

Any question as to whether or not they were to be vigilantes was quickly answered when they were seen patrolling the town with Edge Dunn.

Within two days after the "law enforcement committee" was organized, Dodge City got its first look at the vigilantes in action.

Four Buffalo hunters, unaware that any such committee had been formed, were in the Alhambra Saloon. Having recently sold their hides, their pockets were full of money, and they were drunk. They decided to celebrate, and the celebration was beginning to get out of hand.

"Hey, Hog Jaw," one of them called to his friend. "Why don't we give these folks an 'exhibition'? Let's show 'em some real shootin'."

"How we goin' to do that, Stubby?"

"Hell, it'll be easy," Stubby said. "We'll line us up a bunch o' whisky glasses up on the piano, then we'll shoot 'em off the top."

"No, now, don't you boys be doin' nothin' like that," the bartender said. "You can't go shootin' guns off in here."

"Ahh, don't worry none about it," Stubby said with a dismissive wave of his hand. "As long as the bullets go where we want 'em to go, there ain't goin' to be no problems."

Even as Stubby was talking, Hog Jaw put a glass on top of the piano.

"Now, watch this," Stubby said. He fired at the glass and shattered it cleanly, with no sign of his bullet hitting the piano, though it did punch a hole through the back wall.

"Now it's my turn," Hog Jaw said.

"Billy Ray," the bartender said, quietly. "Go get the vigilantes."

Billy Ray sneaked out of the saloon without his departure being noticed by either Stubby or Hog Jaw, then he hurried down the street and across the tracks.

Edge Dunn had taken a small building on the south side of the railroad tracks for his office. The building had been a land agency, but Dunn ran the agent off. He was enjoying a cigar while sitting in what had been the agent's chair, with his feet propped up on what had been the agent's desk, when Billy Ray came in.

"Sheriff?"

"I ain't no sheriff."

"But you're like one, ain't you? I mean if we need a sheriff, ain't we s'posed to come to you?"

"What's it that you need a sheriff for?"

"Stubby 'n Hog Jaw . . .they're a couple of buffalo hunters, 'n they're shootin' up down at Mr. Kelley's bar is what they're a' doin'."

"All right, I'll go take care of 'em."

As Dunn started for the Alhambra in a swift stride, Billy Ray had to quicken his step to keep pace.

"I figure if you just go in there 'n talk to 'em," Billy Ray said. "I mean, just tell 'em that you're the law now, 'n they can't come into a place just raisin' hell, no more."

Dunn didn't answer. They heard another shot coming from the saloon, not the flat, loud shot of a pistol, but the roaring thunder of a buffalo gun.

Dunn reached the saloon first and he pushed right on in through the batwing doors. Stubby had just fired, and was pulling the empty shell casing from his Sharps .50. Hog Jaw was raising his rifle to his shoulder.

The patrons of the saloon, who had moved to the extreme sides of the room so as not to be in the path of the two drunken shooters had their fingers stuck into their ears, waiting for the next shot.

But instead of one shot, there were two shots, and they came from Dunn's pistol. Stubby was shot in the chest, and Hog Jaw in the back. Both men went down.

"What the hell?" the bartender shouted. "You just shot both of 'em!"

"Yeah," Dunn said, turning to leave the saloon. "I reckon they won't be givin' you no more trouble now, will they?"

Within days, the town became, noticeably, more peaceful.

"I didn't know how this was goin' to be, but it's working out real good. Why, I haven't even had a fight in my saloon since them boys come, let alone a shootin'," Mo Waters said.

"Still," Herman Fringer said, shaking his head. "There's something about this whole vigilante thing that's making me mighty uneasy."

"You were against it from the beginning," Frederic Zimmerman said. "The vigilantes could start holding come to Jesus meetings, and you still wouldn't like it."

"Still, I don't care; I don't have a good feeling about this," Fringer repeated.

Shortly before the vigilante committee was formed a new saloon, The Railroad Saloon, was built. It was in a prime location on South Front Street, which ran parallel to the railroad but south of the tracks, whereas most of the established businesses were north of the tracks. The saloon had no connection to the Atchison, Topeka and Santa Fe, but one couldn't tell that from just looking at it. Mr.

Dunham and Mr. Dawson had gone to great pains to make it look like a depot. It was the newest saloon in town and the buffalo hunters, soldiers, and railroad workers were flocking to it in ever increasing numbers.

One reason for the saloon's success was that the women the owners had brought in charged less to go upstairs with their customers than either the Devil's Den or Fat Tom Sherman's Dance Hall.

For a while, the Slaters were willing to let the saloon be in peace, but the Railroad Saloon was getting bigger and more successful, and more significantly, it's increase in business was coming at the expense of business at the Devil's Den.

It was for this reason that Mack, Luke, and Weasel were having a serious discussion with Edge Dunn.

"You've been doin' a real good job," Luke said. "The town's just got real peaceful."

"Ain't that what you wanted?" Dunn asked. "Or did you want somethin' else?"

"What do you mean?"

"I figured that maybe, you puttin' me in charge 'n all, that you might of have somethin' else in mind."

Mack smiled, than looked at his two brothers. "I told you Edge would be perfect for the job."

"And now, you got that somethin' else, ain't that right?" Dunn picked up his beer and took a drink.

"Yes, I think we've got a problem," Mack said. "Did you know that Dunham's got whores down at the Railroad Saloon? Whores, mind you, in a town that's supposed to be cleaned up."

"Wait a minute, you ain't sayin' we were supposed to run all the whores out." Dunn was confused by the direction of the conversation.

"No, no Mr. Dunn. I want only Mr. Dunham's whores run out."

"It ain't goin' to work," Dunn said. "That is unless we do it permanent."

"Then maybe you should think of a way to make it permanent."

Dunn nodded, then drained the rest of his beer.

"I'll take Digger and Rocky with me,"

When Dunn stepped into the saloon, the two vigilantes with him were each carrying a wad of cloth. If someone had been close enough to the two men, they might have gotten a whiff of kerosene, though the other smells in the saloon, tobacco smoke, unwashed bodies, stale whiskey, and a strong aroma of the perfume being worn by the girls, made it somewhat less likely.

Dunn recognized several of the men who had previously patronized the Devil's Den. Seeing Dunn, many of these men looked away to keep from staring at him.

"Edge Dunn," a big man said from behind the bar. This was Ira Dunham, one of the owners of the Railroad Saloon, and he was speaking around a half-chewed cigar that was stuck in the corner of his mouth. "I thought you was a Devil's Den man. What brings you to the Railroad Saloon?"

"You might 'a heard, I got me a new job," Dunn said.

"I did see that in the paper. You're chief of the vigilantes, I believe."

"Yes."

"That's mighty big of you to take that on, seein' as how you don't make no money."

"The Slaters still pays me. He says he's doin' it for the town."

Dunham nodded his head. "Uh huh, 'n now that brings me back to the same question I asked when you first come in. What ya doin' in here? We ain't had no trouble."

"Your whores."

Dunham smiled. "Yeah, they're some dandies all right. I went all the way to Philadelphia to bring 'em out here, and they're a hell of a lot better lookin' than them rundown whores that's at Devil's Den. You come here to try 'em out, did you?"

"No, I came here to tell you you're goin' to have to get rid of 'em.," Dunn said.

"What do you mean?"

"Whores is against the law in Dodge City."

"Since when did that happen?" Dunham asked "And for that matter, when have we had laws in this town, anyway?"

"I'm the law," Dunn said in a quiet, but menacing voice. "And I'm tellin' you, your whores is illegal."

"Well tell me, Mr. Lawman, will you be runnin' the whores out of Devil's Den and Fat Tom's Dance Hall as well?"

"That ain't none of your worry," Dunn said.

"Why don't we have a drink 'n talk about this a little more?" Dunham reached under the bar but instead of bringing up a whiskey bottle, he brought up a shotgun.

"Now get outta my saloon you son of a . . ."

That was as far as he got before a pistol appeared in Dunn's hand. He fired as soon as he brought the gun up and Dunham was driven back against the mirror behind the bar. With the shotgun pointing straight up, he pulled the trigger in a reflexive action, then slid down to the floor, leaving a smear of blood on the mirror.

The roar of the two gunshots brought an immediate quiet to what had earlier been a very animated gathering of drinkers.

"What the hell, Dunn, you just kilt Dunham! What'd you do that for?" one of the patrons asked in a stunned voice, putting to words what everyone else was thinking.

"This here saloon is closed," Dunn said.

"Closed for how long?" one of the patrons asked.

"Forever."

"Closed?" one of the soiled doves said. "What do you mean closed? What do we do now?"

"I don't care what you do now," Dunn replied. "But maybe you might want to catch the next train back to Philadelphia." As he was talking, the two men who had come in with him began hanging the cloth, which turned out to be kerosene soaked quilts.

Then they took a couple of the kerosene lanterns, opened the fuel tanks, and began sprinkling the kerosene on the bar.

"What the hell are you men a' doin' there?" someone asked.

Digger and Rocky began striking matches, and touching them to the quilts they had nailed to the walls.

"Son of a bitch, they've set fire to the place," someone shouted. "Get out! Ever' one get out! This place 'll burn fast."

As if validating the warning, the flames leaped back and forth between the bar to the wall behind, and within seconds so much of the saloon was invested in flames that everyone knew it would be impossible to put it out. Smoke rolled up the stairway, and from the top floor there were screams.

"Hey, they's a couple of women up there!" someone said, and braving the smoke-filled stairway, he ran up to the second floor.

When Edge Dunn and the two vigilantes left the saloon they were the last to do so, and they pushed their way through the crowd that had been drawn by the fire. They were barely noticed by the men and women whose attention was now focused on the building that was totally engulfed in flames.

Mack and Luke Slater were standing in front of the Devil's Den, looking down the street toward the Railroad Saloon when Edge and the other two men came up to them.

"We need a drink," Dunn said.

"It's on the house," Mack replied, not taking his eyes off the burning building.

"It's not fair," Lola Fontaine said, later that same day.

"What's not fair?" Mack asked.

"It's not fair that my girls don't make any money when they're with the vigilantes."

"It's what they're paying for protection. Hell, look at it from our point of view. We get half of what the girls get, 'n when they're layin' with one of the vigilantes, we don't get nothin' for it neither. Besides," he added with a broad smile, "business is bound to pick up for 'em now, seein' as how there ain't no more competition from down at The Railroad Saloon."

"Folks are sayin' you ordered Dunn to burn the saloon down," Lola said. "Is that true?"

"It ain't, but I have to say, it was a good idea."

"Mack, you, 'n your brothers have a real good thing goin' here. Me too, for that matter. But if you get the whole town down on you, I'm afraid they're going get their fill of it and run you out of town."

"Ah, don't worry your pretty head none about it," Mack said. "I know what I'm doin'. Pretty soon now I'll have this town eatin' out of the palm of my hand. They won't nobody do nothin', without first I tell 'em they can do it."

The editor of the *Dodge City Messenger*, looked at the plate reading the story he had just set. The words were reversed, but Pat Marsh had been in the newspaper business long enough to be able to read backward type as easily as he could read the finished product. He knew that this story may not be taken well in some areas of town, but it was a story that he felt needed to be told.

> *The Railroad Saloon Fire*
> *Citizens of the town became aware last week of the fire that consumed The Railroad Hotel. It is worth noting that although no effort was made to extinguish the flames, such an effort would have been futile, so quickly did the fire take hold.*
> *It is obvious that the rapid expansion of the fire was the result of an accelerant, and that suggests that the fire might well be the result of arson. This newspaper has*

interviewed several who were in the saloon at the time of the fire, but not one will testify that they witnessed the fire being set.

It can be inferred, however, from bits and pieces of conversation gleaned from first one witness, then another, that the chief of our "law enforcement committee" and two of his "vigilantes" (for indeed, that is what they are) might well be the perpetrators of this arson. Though no one has made that direct accusation, it is known that they arrived shortly before the fire began, the fire erupted while they were there, and grew to a conflagration by the time they left.

Five people died in the fire, the victims being two unidentified buffalo hunters, and Bessie and Jill, two of the 'soiled doves' who worked there. The four were upstairs engaged in that activity that so frequently draws men to women of such ilk. The fifth victim was Ira Dunham himself, the owner of the saloon who ascended the stairs in an attempt to give warning.

Is this what our city's board of directors and businessmen voted for, to empower these vigilantes to hold sway over us? It is the fear of this newspaper, dear readers, that we have unleashed the tiger. No good can come to Dodge City as long as the vigilantes are allowed to roam

> *our streets, under the guise of authority, wielding their brand of justice.*

Two days after that article was printed, the Washington Hand Press, by which Marsh printed his papers, wound up on its side, the type spread all around. Marsh got the message.

Chapter Twenty-Six

CADE WAS IN the lot looking over the mules, when Jeter came out of the office, holding a piece of paper. By the way he was striding so purposefully toward him, Cade knew that it had to be something important. And by the way Jeter was smiling, though, he knew that it wasn't bad news.

"Jeter, what is it?"

"What would you say if I told you we had a twenty-five hundred dollar contract?"

"Are you kidding? That would be great! What will we be carrying?"

"All the telegram says is military supplies," Jeter said, brandishing the piece of paper. "But Colonel Dodge wants us to come out to the post today, and meet with him."

***

The bugler was playing *Retreat,* and the flag was being struck as Cade, Jeter, and Jacob rode onto the post

229

at four o'clock that afternoon. The three men dismounted and stood respectfully until the flag was removed from the lanyard, and the color detail began folding it into the tricorn. When they stepped into the post headquarters building, a soldier with a mop and pail moved to one side to let them pass.

"We were asked to call on Colonel Dodge," Cade said. "Is it too late to see him?"

"No sir, the colonel's still here. He's expecting you," Sergeant Major Dawes replied.

As the sergeant major stepped into the colonel's office Cade glanced toward the soldier on detail, the mop making very lazy swaths across the floor.

"Careful you don't run a hole through the wood there," Cade teased.

The soldier looked up at him, the expression on his face indicating clearly that he didn't appreciate the joke.

A moment later, Sergeant Major Dawes opened the door to the colonel's office.

"The colonel will see you now."

"Good, good, you got the message I see," Dodge said, greeting the three at the door. Come in, Gentlemen, come in."

The soldier mopping the floor of the headquarters was Private Lemon. He had been promoted to corporal after he had returned from the horse delivery detail with a bullet in his shoulder. He had told the story of how he, Sergeant Gulliver and the others had tried to fight off the horse thieves. There had been too many of them, and he was the only one to live through the attack having survived by pretending to be dead.

For a short while Lemon enjoyed the accolades of the post, but his promotion to corporal didn't last very long. And now he was on punishment detail for being insubordinate to the new stable sergeant.

Lemon had been looking for another bit of information he could sell to Fargo, and when he saw that Colonel Dodge had not closed the door completely, he moved his mop pail close enough to be able to overhear what was being said inside.

There were chairs enough for all of them in the colonel's office, and Cade, Jeter, and Jacob accepted Colonel Dodge's invitation to take a seat.

"Gentlemen, what I am about to tell you is secret information. But, as it involves you, or at least, I hope it involves you, I would think that you have a valid need to know."

"This has to do with the twenty-five hundred dollar contract?" Cade asked.

"Oh, indeed it does, Mr. McCall, indeed it does. I hope that you have the sand for it." Colonel Dodge paused for a moment, then looked each of them in eyes before he continued.

"One week from now, we are expecting a rail shipment of the brand-new Springfield Trapdoor Model 73 rifles. There will be two hundred fifty of them along with two hundred thousand rounds of .45 caliber bullets. I need these rifles and that ammunition to be taken to Camp Supply."

Jacob let out a little whistle. "Wouldn't the Indians love to get their hands on those babies?"

"It's not just Indians. We're finding that white road agents are becoming more and more brazen. They'd have an instant outlet for these weapons if they were able to get their hands on them," Colonel Dodge said.

"All three of us are flattered that you have brought this contract to us, but I have to ask. Why is it, with such a sensitive shipment, you are not using one of the bigger freighting companies?" Cade asked. "Charlie Rath's company or even Reynolds and Lee. They both put dozens of wagons on the road, and we only have four."

"It's for the very reason that you are small that we have chosen you. We don't think anyone would suspect that we would ship this kind of cargo with you."

"Well, we appreciate your trust in us," Cade said. "We'll do our best to see that these rifles get to Camp Supply."

"Nobody on the post knows about this yet, and nobody will know until the day the shipment gets here. I plan for us to take the rifles from the train, load them onto your wagons, and for you to leave, on the same day. That will keep any chance of news getting out about the shipment to an absolute minimum."

"I can also see why the army is offering to pay so much for this contract. The drivers will be taking a big risk."

"I understand that," Colonel Dodge said. "Now I hope you can see why there's such a need for secrecy."

"Yes, sir, Colonel, indeed we can," Jacob said.

"All right, gentlemen, you now know what I'm asking of you. So the question is, are you willing to take the contract?"

Cade, Jeter, and Jacob glanced at each other, and that glance was all they needed. The three men gave a quick nod, and Jacob responded for them all.

"We are," he said.

"Very good, gentlemen, the army thanks you, and I thank you," Colonel Dodge said. He stood and started toward the door. "I'll see you next week."

By the time the three men left Colonel Dodge's office, Lemon, having heard all he needed to hear, had moved his mop and pail to the opposite side of the room.

"If you three men want to remain on the post for dinner, I'll send word to the officers' mess to expect you," Sergeant Major Dawes said.

"That's thoughtful of you, Sergeant Major, but we'd better get back to town."

"Yes, sir," Dawes replied.

"Hey, Sergeant Major, can I go now? I've got the whole floor mopped, and Sergeant Caviness is lookin' for me in the stables," Lemon said.

"Go ahead," Dawes said without looking up.

"Thanks."

After *Taps*, that evening, while some were sleeping and others were playing cards in the barracks, Private Al Lemon got out of his bunk, left the barracks, and went to the stables to saddle a horse. As there was no stockade fence around Fort Dodge, it was easy for him to leave the post.

"Al, what are you doing here? And you aren't even in uniform," Rosalie said, when the young man stepped into the Devil's Den. Rosalie was one of the soiled doves who had become Al Lemon's favorite. She was a quadroon, with a smooth, golden-toned skin that gave her an exotic beauty.

"I ain't in the army no more."

"What? What did you do? I thought you said you'd be here for a year."

"I decided I didn't want to wait a year."

Rosalie's eyes got big. "You deserted! Al, you can't stay here, someone will see you and they'll find you."

"I ain't goin' to stay aroun', but I couldn't leave without tellin' my favorite girl goodbye, now, could I?" He smiled at her.

"You don't fool me, Al. Any girl that you've got money for is your favorite girl." Rosalie kissed him.

"I have to see Fargo. Is he here?"

"Yeah, he went up with Dolly about a half hour ago."

"A half hour? It don't never take me that long," Lemon complained.

Rosalie laughed. "It sure don't, honey."

"There he is, now," Al said, as he went to meet Fargo at the bottom of the stairs.

"Damn, Lemon, what are you doin' here and out of uniform?" Fargo asked.

"I ain't never gonna wear that uniform again."

Fargo sighed. "What have you done this time?"

Lemon smiled. "Wait 'til you hear what I've got tonight. I won't never need the army again."

"I'm thinking that for a job that's this important we should take it ourselves," Cade said the next morning. He, Jeter, and Jacob were discussing the delivery of the rifles to Camp Supply.

"I agree," Jeter said. "This is a high-risk trip, and after what happened to Lambdin and Morris, I wouldn't feel right putting it off on our drivers."

"Because it's such a high risk, I don't think we should try and take it without guards," Jacob said.

"I agree," Cade said, "but because of the danger involved, I think we should ask for volunteers to ride as shotgun and then pay them double."

"That would work, but don't tell them about the pay until after they volunteer," Jeter said.

"It won't be fair if we don't tell them what the cargo is," Jacob said.

"Let's hold off on that," Cade said. "Remember what Colonel Dodge said. We have to keep this a secret, and we can't take a chance on word of it getting out ahead of time. At first, we'll just tell them that the trip could be very dangerous."

"I'll bring the men in," Jeter said.

Fifteen minutes later all six employees of Harrison, McCall and Willis were crowded into the little office.

"What's up, Boss?" Cahill asked.

"You mean bosses, don't you?" Foster asked.

"Yeah, it must be somethin' big, bein' as all three of 'em are here," Keaton said.

"Men," Cade began. "We have a trip coming up that can be, well, I don't want lie to you, but it can be very dangerous."

"How dangerous?" Pullen asked.

"Extremely dangerous," Cade replied, and all the drivers looked at each other.

"Because of that," Cade said, speaking quickly before any other questions could be asked, "Jacob, Jeter, and I will be taking the trip ourselves."

"Wait a minute," Cahill said. "If it's all that dangerous, why would the three of you go all by yourselves?"

Cade smiled. "When I say we would be taking the trip ourselves, I didn't say we would be going off alone. And that's part of the reason for this meeting. I'm going to ask for three volunteers to come along as outriders for the wagons."

"I'll go," Cahill said, without hesitation. "I'll ride alongside Jeter's wagon, seein' as how me 'n him have been workin' together so long."

"Thanks, Pete," Jeter said.

The other five men looked at each other. Three of the remaining five were married, and there was a hesitation before Pullen spoke up. He was one of the two remaining unmarried men.

"I'll go."

"I will too," Foster said. Foster was married.

"You're married, Foster, are you sure you want to do this?" Jeter asked.

Foster smiled. "Well, hell, boss, you're married too, ain't you?"

Jeter returned the smile.

"All right, Cahill, Pullen, and Foster, you stay here for a couple of minutes so we can get this trip all planned out. The rest of you can get on back to what you were doing."

After the other three left, those who remained looked expectantly toward Cade.

"What is it about this trip that's making it so dangerous?" Cahill asked.

Cade shook his head. "Huh, uh, I can't tell you yet. But I will tell you when we pick up the load."

"All right."

"Here's another thing," Cade said. "Each of you will be getting double pay for this trip. I didn't want to mention it before, because I didn't want you to volunteer just based upon the extra money you would be receiving."

The three men exchanged smiles.

"Mr. Harrison," Foster said. "Uh, if somethin' was to happen to me, I mean, seein' as how dangerous it is, 'n all, would you see to it that my wife gets the money that would'a been comin' to me?"

"I tell you what, Foster, suppose I give you your money now, and you can give it to your wife before we leave?" Jacob suggested.

Foster shook his head. "No, sir. If I was to do that, she'd worry somethin' fierce. I'd rather you give it to her after the trip is over, if, for some reason, I don't get back."

"Here's a better idea," Jeter said. "Let's just all get back."

The others laughed.

Chapter Twenty-Seven

LUKE, WEASEL, Dunn, Dutch Henry, Fargo, and three more vigilantes rode out of Dodge raising the curiosity of the citizens of the town as they saw them all leaving in a group. They saw another man join them at the edge of town.

"Where do ya think there a goin'? one of the citizens asked.

"Maybe they're leaving town," another one said, as he chuckled.

"We wouldn't be so lucky."

"Oh, now don't be so hard on 'em. They did stop most of the violence." another suggested.

"Stop the violence, like hell. They just took it over."

Back at the Devil's Den, Lola was looking at the ledger she kept for the girls who worked there. Since the Slaters had taken on the job of supporting the vigilantes, the income generated by the girls had dropped drastically. Ironically, they were now busier than they had ever been, but for much of the time they didn't make any money because they were expected to entertain the vigilantes for free.

Rosalie was sitting at Lola's table discussing the vigilante problem.

"At least we don't have to deal with so many of them today," Rosalie said. "Where are they, anyway?" she asked.

"Who?"

"Dunn and his men. They're gone, or at least half of 'em are."

"That's strange," Lola said. "Luke and Weasel are gone too, but I don't have any idea where they are."

"The longer they're gone the better, as far as I'm concerned," Rosalie said.

"Miss Lola, Miss Lola, you've got to help me!" Cetti said, hurrying up to Lola's table.

"What is it?"

"It's Shardeen. Frankie says he's lookin' for me again."

"Shardeen," Rosalie said. She spit as she said his name. "He's the worst one."

"Then we need to get Cetti out of here. The only thing is, I don't know where to put her."

"I know somewhere," Rosalie said.

"You do?"

"Yes, it's someone I knew a long time ago. She'll hide Cetti; I know she will."

"Who is it? No, wait, don't tell me. If I don't know where Cetti is, I can't give it away."

"Come on, Cetti," Rosalie said.

"I'll just get my . . ." Cetti started, but Rosalie interrupted her in mid-sentence.

"No, come on, now, before Shardeen knows you're missing."

Rosalie took the young girl across the track, then down to Fourth Avenue. Then hurrying up Fourth Avenue she reached the corner house.

"I know who lives here," Cetti said as they walked up to the house. "This is the lady with the two little girls."

"Yes," Rosalie answered, as she knocked on the door.

An older woman answered the knock. Rosalie was wearing the dress and makeup of her profession, and seeing the young woman Mary Hatley took a step back in surprise.

"Is Magnolia here? I mean, uh, Mrs. Willis?" Rosalie asked.

"She is."

"Tell her it's someone she knew from before. From *Le plaisir d'un Gentleman*."

"Did I hear you say you knew me from New Orleans? I don't remember you," Magnolia said, having come to the front door just in time to hear Rosalie. "Who are you?"

"Here I'm Rosalie, but you knew me by the name my mama gave me. She called me Antoinette."

"Antoinette? Wait a minute, was your mother Gabrielle?"

Rosalie smiled.

"I do remember you, but you were just a child, not much older than this one."

"This is Cetti," Rosalie said. "And she's the reason I'm here. Miss Magnolia, please, you have to help her. If we don't get her away from the..." she paused for a moment, then spat out a word that could almost be profanity, "vigilantes . . . I don't know what will happen to her. Please, will you help?"

"Of course I will," Maggie agreed. "Get her in here."

When Rosalie returned to the saloon, Mack was talking to Lola, and Frankie.

"Where is she?" Mack asked.

"That's what I'd like to know," Frankie replied. "Mr. Slater, help me find my sister, I'm afraid she's run away."

"Now why would she do that? She's got a nice place to stay here."

"I don't know, but I'm scared. She's only sixteen years old; she don't know how to take care of herself. You gotta help me find her."

"She's a little fool, now that's what she is," Mack said. He smiled. "I know you ain't let her be with a man. Why, I could hold an auction this very day, and sell her to any man who steps foot through that door. There ain't no tellin' how much money that would have brought, 'n I'd a give Cetti half of it."

Frankie shook her head. "I'm hoping she never goes into the business."

"Nonsense, look how good it's been for you," Mack said. "Cetti's a pretty thing. She'll find out she can't do no better than workin' right here at the Devil's Den. You mark my words, she'll be slinkin' back in here, and when she does, why she's gonna have to earn her keep. No more of this cleanin' stuff." Mack turned and walked away.

Frankie looked at Rosalie with questioning eyes.

"Everything is fine," Rosalie whispered.

"Thank you," Frankie said. "From the bottom of my heart, I thank you."

At that very moment, Luke and the others were waiting at the ford of the Cimarron River in Indian Territory. It had rained for three days, and the water was up.

"Lemon, you're sure now that these here wagons is carryin' guns?" Weasel asked. "I'm goin' to be some upset if we take the wagons 'n find there ain't nothin' in 'em but flour."

"Yeah, I'm sure. I heard the colonel himself tell 'em that they'd be carryin' two hunnert 'n fifty rifles 'n two hunnert thousand bullets," Lemon said.

Luke smiled. "Damn! You got 'ny idea what we can get from this? I'm thinkin' we can take 'em down to New Mexico to the Comancheros. We'd get a hell of a lot more money than we could get from anybody around here, and the guns would be outta here."

"How you plannin' on pullin' this off, Luke?" Dunn asked.

"I figure soon as they come around the bend, we'll commence a' shootin'," Luke replied.

Dunn shook his head. "That ain't the way to do it."

"How would you do it?" Luke asked, a little piqued by Dunn's response.

"This here is the only place they can ford the river, 'n they're goin' to have to do it just real slow and careful what with the water up and all," Dunn replied. "If it was up to me, I'd wait until they are about half way across, then we'll ambush 'em."

"Yeah," Luke agreed. "That's a good idea. 'n if we shoot the mules when they're comin' acrost, why, we'll have 'em trapped."

242

"Don't shoot the mules," Weasel said. "If you do, how we gonna haul away the guns?"

"All right, we won't shoot the mules."

Cade was driving the first wagon, and when they reached the river he stopped.

"What is it, Cade?" Pullen was on horseback, riding alongside the wagon.

"I don't know," Cade said. His rifle was in the foot-well of the wagon, and he reached for it.

Cade thought he had seen something on the other side of the river, but he couldn't say for sure that he had. He didn't know if he was reacting on something he had seen, or something he was feeling.

"Trade places with me, Pullen, you drive the wagon and let me have the horse."

"All right," Pullen agreed and the switch was made. "You want me to start across the river?"

"No, hold up. I want to talk this over with the others."

Cade rode back to a curious Jeter and Jacob. Jacob was driving the second wagon, but Jeter, who was in the third wagon, had jumped down and was standing alongside when Cade came back to them.

"What's going on, Cade?"

"If we're going to be hit, it'll be right here, while we're crossing the Cimarron," Cade said. "I think we should be ready for anything."

"I have a suggestion," Jeter said. "Remember at Shiloh when Forrest had us bring the wagons up all together? We could do that here so all three wagons are side by side. That way if we're hit, we'll have our maximum strength organized."

"A good idea, for a Johnny Reb," Jacob said, as he pulled his wagon up to the right side of Cade's wagon.

"Just watch your mouth, Harrison." Jeter was laughing as he walked back to his own wagon.

"Now what?" Jacob asked when the wagons were three abreast, facing the river.

Cade, who was holding his rifle in his right hand, stroked his chin with his left as he studied the other side.

Weasel was certain he hadn't been seen, so what was holding them up? Why didn't they come on across?

"What is it?" he asked. "What are they a' doin'?"

"It looks like Mr. Cade McCall has got hisself a notion," Dutch Henry said.

"So, what do we do?"

"We kill 'im," Dunn said.

Dunn raised his rifle drew a sight on Cade's head, then began, slowly to tighten his finger on the trigger.

Seeing that the bit had repositioned slightly, and in a way that might be uncomfortable for the horse, Cade bent over to reposition it. As he did so, he heard the crack rifle-fire, and felt his hat fly off his head.

"Cade!" Jeter shouted in alarm.

Cade leaped down from his horse. "Get down!" he called. "All of you on the ground!"

The other five men abandoned horse and wagon, and all six of them took up a prone position on the north side of the river. Cade lined up his sight on a target, and pulled the trigger. A man fell forward, pushing the scrub willows aside, exposing another. Jeter took out the man who was exposed.

"Dunn, do somethin'!" someone yelled from across the river. "They got Dutch Henry and Carter!"

The man's shout was followed by a volley of fire from the other side of the river.

For the next few minutes there was a brisk exchange of gunfire.

"Uhh!" Pullen called out, and glancing toward him Cade saw that he had been badly hit.

Another of the ambushers was hit.

"I don't know how many they've got, but we've taken care of three of them now," Foster said.

"They got Dunn!" someone shouted from across the river.

"Dunn?" Jeter said. "That has to be Edge. You don't think this is the work of the vigilantes?"

"It wouldn't surprise me. We've seen what kind of men they are, and a gun shipment has to be an attractive target."

"But how did they find out?"

"I don't have any idea. All I know is, we didn't tell."

"Weasel," Luke said crawling toward his brother. "We gotta get out of here."

"And leave all them guns?"

"They's only five of us left, 'n that means they got us outnumbered. No way we're goin' to get them guns now."

"Damn, I hate lettin' 'em go."

"Then you go get 'em," Luke said. "But me, I'm gettin' out of here."

***

"Come back here, you bastards!" The man who had called out was yelling at a couple of riders going up the hill, though from this side of the river, Cade couldn't see them well enough to identify them.

"Digger! Get down you fool!" a voice called from behind the bushes.

The one called Digger turned and began firing his rifle toward Cade and the others. Though he was exposed, he was also dangerous, because he was coming very close, one of the bullets kicking sand into Cade's face.

Several of Cade's men fired, and Digger went down.

Over the next few minutes, the volume of fire dropped off sharply then all firing stopped on both sides of the river.

"How many of you are left?" Cade called across to them.

There was no answer, but a single shot was fired.

"You know what I think?" Cade called. "I think there're no more than two of you. You have two, and we have six. If you're after my cargo, you know damn well there's no way you're going to get it."

Another shot was fired.

"Come out where we can see you," Cade said. "Drop your guns and throw your hands up, and we'll let you live."

For a long moment there was no response.

"If that's the way you want it, just know you're going to die right here, today," Cade warned.

"All right, all right, we're comin' out."

A couple of rifles were tossed from the bushes, then two men appeared with their hands raised.

"Well, will you look at that," Cade said. "The mop boy."

"I guess we know how they found out about the rifles," Jeter said.

"That other feller goes by the name of Fargo," Cahill said. "He used to come into the Dodge House, from time to time."

"Cade?" Jacob said in a quiet voice. Jacob was squatted down beside Pullen. "Pullen's dead."

"Damn," Cade said. "Go over and get those two murdering bastards and if either one of them moves a muscle, shoot his ass."

When Cahill and Foster brought the two across the river, Cade went down to the river to meet them.

"I should put a bullet in you right now, but I'll let the US Army take care of you. At the very least you're going to be facing a murder charge."

"We're not the only ones," Fargo said.

"Oh, who else?"

"Luke 'n Weasel Slater. Them two cowardly bastards is the ones that planned this, then they run away, leavin' me 'n Fargo 'n Digger behind, only, you done kilt Digger. And I ain't goin' to face no murder charge with what they don't neither," Lemon said.

"Wait, there're riders comin'," Cahill said training his rifle across the river.

"Maybe it's the Slaters coming back," Jeter said.

"Looks like a whole bunch of 'em. It's soldiers," Cahill said.

"One of the army patrols out of Camp Supply," Jacob said.

Lieutenant Feller was in charge of the detail of twenty men, and when he saw the wagons stopped, he hurried forward crossing the river.

"Any trouble here?"

"We were attacked," Cade said. He nodded toward Fargo and Lemon.

"These two?"

"There were more. You'll find the bodies back there," Jacob said pointing to the other side of the river. "And from what this one said, two got away."

"I was told I would be meeting a shipment from Fort Dodge," Lieutenant Feller said. "Did you see anything on the road?

"Yes, sir, we would be the shipment you are expecting." Cade took in the three wagons with a wave.

"Uh." the Lieutenant had a perplexed look on his face. "I don't think so. What I was expecting was very valuable cargo. I'm sure the colonel would have provided a fairly large detail to accompany it."

"Follow me, Lieutenant," Cade said. He walked back to the first wagon and raised the canvas. "Is this what you're expecting?"

The lieutenant's mouth dropped open. "You five men brought this all by yourself?"

"No, there were six of us, but we'll be burying one," Jacob said.

"I'm sorry," the lieutenant said. "My orders are to escort this shipment onto Camp Supply. I'm sure you know that going through the Territory, this cargo cannot fall into the wrong hands."

"We can appreciate that. We'd also like you to take these men into custody."

"I don't have any authority to do that. They're civilians."

"All right, I'll kill them," Cade said, and raising his pistol he pulled back the hammer."

"No, wait! Lieutenant, I'm Private Lemon. I'm in the army. I deserted!"

"Yeah, me too! I'm Corporal Fargo!"

"Too late," Cade said. "You heard the lieutenant. He doesn't want you."

"Hold it," Lieutenant Feller said. "I suppose, I mean seeing as how they both say they're army deserters, I would have the authority to take charge of them."

Cade eased the hammer back down, then returned the pistol to his holster.

"I thought you might. Since we've got an army escort for the rest of the way, I'd like to leave now, so I can get Pullen back to town."

"That's not the only reason you want to leave. You're going after the Slaters, aren't you?" Jeter asked.

"I am. You comin' with me?"

Jeter smiled. "You're damn right, I am."

Chapter Twenty-Eight

BAT MASTERSON was just coming out of the Alhambra when he saw Cade and Jeter riding back into town. They were leading a third horse, over which was draped a body. Knowing they would be headed for the mortuary, he hurried down to meet them.

Lola was standing at the front of the saloon, looking out over the top of the batwing doors when she saw Cade and Jeter riding into town, leading a horse with a body.

"They're bringing in a dead man," she said.

"Who?" Rosalie asked.

"I don't know but that's Mr. McCall and Mr. Willis bringin' him in."

"I wonder what happened?" Rosalie asked, stepping over to look outside.

"You two, quit gawking and get to work," Luke said.

"Too bad he didn't stay away like the others did," Rosalie said under her breath as she moved away from the door.

Of those who left a few days earlier, only Luke and Weasel had returned, and without any word as to what had happened to the others.

Lola didn't know what the trip was about, or why the others didn't come back, but when Luke and Weasel returned, she knew that Mack was most upset about it. The three brothers had a discussion and to say that the discussion was spirited would have been an understatement, since there were frequent, and very loud invectives hurled between them.

Lola had not been able to gather from the shouts and cursing, what it was about, but she believed it had something to do with a missed opportunity of some sort.

When someone came into town, belly down on the saddle, it got everyone's attention, and word spread down the street faster than the leisurely advance of the horses. As a result, Eb Collar was standing out in front of his establishment when Cade and Jeter rode up.

"Who you got here?" Collar asked.

"Abraham Pullen. He's one of our drivers," Cade said.

"Has he family?"

"He has a brother back in Missouri. I'd like you to prepare the body so it can be shipped back. I'll get you the address from our office records."

"All right," Collar said.

"Cade, what happened?" Bat asked.

"We were delivering guns," Cade answered. "We were attacked just before we crossed the Cimarron."

"What fool sends guns through the Indian Territory, or I should say what fools take on cargo like that?"

"To answer your question, the second fools would be us and the first fools would be the US Army," Cade said.

"You got to be kidding," Bat said. "That's suicide. Did you get the guns through?"

"I guess so. Jacob and the boys took them on to Camp Supply, but they had an army escort, so if they lost them, it's the blue boys that did it."

"Getting back to the attack. Did they catch the perpetrators?"

"We had a pretty good little battle and we killed most of 'em," Jeter said. "The two that were left turned out to be deserters, so the lieutenant . . . after some powerful persuasion from Cade, agreed to take them.

But the ringleaders got away."

"Damn, that's always the way it is. It's the little guys who take the brunt," Bat said.

"We know who they are," Jeter said. "We saw two men riding away while the battle was going on, and if I'd have known who they were, I would have risked everything to kill the sons of bitches with my own hands."

"Well, who was it?"

"Our old nemeses, the Slaters. It's no telling where those bastards are now," Cade said.

Bat smiled. "I know where they are."

"Oh?" Jeter replied.

"I saw them no more than an hour ago," Bat said. "All three of them, but I don't know where their henchman is, though."

"Dunn's dead," Cade said flatly, as he pulled his pistol and rotated the cylinder making certain every chamber was full. "I hope he's feeding the buzzards by now."

"Hot damn! You're going after the Slaters, aren't you?" Bat said.

Cade just looked at him and started moving toward the Devil's Den.

"I'm going with you," Bat said as he hurried to catch up with Cade.

"Three against three, that should even the odds a bit," Jeter said as he checked the loads in his own pistol.

"It'll be more than three, Jeter. All the vigilantes weren't at the Cimarron."

"We'll just find out when we get there," Jeter said.

"Jeter, I wish you wouldn't do this. You've got Maggie and the two girls to look after."

"Maggie and one girl," Jeter replied with a smile. "The other one's yours."

Cade nodded. "Yes, she is. All right, gentlemen." Cade took a deep breath. "Let's call on the Slaters."

Lola was sitting at her table when she saw three men step through the front door, then move to the side and begin perusing the room. She recognized them as Cade McCall, Bat Masterson and Jeter Willis. Cade and Bat had been in the Devil's Den before, but she had never ever seen Jeter in the saloon.

Everyone knew the story behind Jeter and the Red House Saloon, so Lola could well understand why he had never been in before. What she didn't know was why he was here now.

Why were any of them here? From the expressions on their faces, she was positive they weren't here for a convivial drink, or a game of poker. Nor did she think any of them would be paying a social call on one of the girls.

Lola glanced toward the bar, where she saw Luke and Weasel. A few minutes ago, Mack had gone upstairs. She had never seen expressions on the Slaters' faces like the ones they wore now. They were expressions of absolute terror.

"Well, now, look what we have here, boys. It looks like Cade McCall 'n a couple of his friends have come to join us," Luke said with a forced bravado.

There were four of the vigilantes still in town, and at the moment, all four were in the saloon. It didn't require any particular math to see that if there was to be a confrontation, the Slaters held a two to one advantage.

Any question that there would be no confrontation was quickly dispelled by Cade's next remark.

"Did you think you could kill one of our drivers, then head for the hills as if nothing had happened?" Cade asked.

"What do you mean kill one of your drivers?" Luke asked.

"You killed Abraham Pullen when you tried to steal the rifles."

"You think you can prove that?" Luke's lips curled into a challenging sneer.

"Prove it?" Cade replied. "What do you mean prove it? I thought you understood."

"You thought I understood what?"

"This isn't a court of law; this is a court of justice, and we don't have to *prove* a damn thing. All we have to do is *know* it. We know you killed Abe, and Slater, you're about to pay for it."

All the time Cade was talking, the vigilantes were beginning to move, opening up the distance between themselves and the Slaters, and themselves and each other.

"I've got the two on the left," Bat said.

"I've got the two on the right," Jeter added.

Cade smiled. "Now, isn't that nice of my friends? They've left you two for me."

There followed a few seconds of silence, broken only by the tick tock of the wall clock.

"Kill 'em!" Luke shouted and his hand started toward his gun. Within the next instant the saloon roared with gunfire. Cade took Luke down first, killing him before he was even able to clear his holster. Because he had turned his attention first to Luke, that had given Weasel an extra beat of time, and he did manage to get his pistol drawn, but when he pulled the trigger the bullet from his gun punched a hole in the floor.

As Cade concentrated on the two Slater brothers, he was aware of the shooting going on beside him, and he glanced left and right to see if either Jeter or Bat needed help. All four of the vigilantes were going down with killing wounds, but Jeter had been hit.

"Jeter!"

"It's in my upper arm," Jeter said with a strained voice. He had already slapped his hand over the wound, but the blood was oozing out between his fingers.

Lola had watched the entire shootout, too stunned by both the immediacy and the ferocity of it to do anything but remain seated at her table. When she saw that Jeter had been hit, she ran over to the bar and grabbed one of the towels then hurried over to the wounded man.

"Here," she said, handing the towel to Cade.

Cade began applying pressure to the wound with the towel. "This'll hold you 'til we can find Fringer."

As Lola stood there beside the two men, she saw, out of the corner of her eye, Mack Slater standing on the upper landing. Mack was pointing a pistol toward Cade.

"Look out!" Lola shouted, pushing Cade away.

Just as Lola made her move, Mack fired, and the bullet hit her high in the chest. Both Cade and Bat returned fire and Mack pitched head first over the rail, did a somersault on the way down, and landed on his back.

Because it was obvious that Mack was dead, Cade and Jeter turned their attention to Lola. It was clear that the wound would be fatal.

"I'm sorry," Lola said, talking only with great difficulty.

"Don't say anything," Cade said as he tried to comfort her.

"I have to. I'm sorry I didn't tell, earlier. I should have told."

"Told what?" Bat asked as he knelt beside Lola.

"I should have told Mr. Willis." Lola gasped for breath, then with great difficulty, continued to talk.

"The I.O.U. wasn't real," she said. "It wasn't for seven thousand two hundred and fifty dollars. It was for two hundred and fifty dollars, but the bet was never even made. The fight began before it could be."

"How do you know this?" Cade asked

"Because I was at the Pig Lot. I saw it all. I'm sorry, I should have..." Lola coughed and when she did, blood came from her mouth. She gasped one more time, then Cade watched as the life left her eyes.

February, 1874

The Red House was back in Jeter's hands, freshly painted and refurbished, considered by many to be the best of the twenty-six saloons in Dodge City. More of a club, than a saloon, it was a place that welcomed men and women, and Magnolia was the gracious hostess.

When Herman and Norma Fringer came in, there were flakes of snow hanging on their hats and clinging to their coats.

"Oh, it's still snowing out there!" Norma said with a shiver as she began to take off her coat.

"Here, let me help you," Magnolia said, holding the shoulders as Norma slipped out of it.

Norma laughed. "The snow doesn't seem to be bothering Mr. McCall and Chantal though."

"What? What do you mean? Are they out there?"

"Step out and see for yourself. He's pulling her up the street on a sled."

"Oh, for heaven's sake he got her that thing for Christmas, and she has hardly gotten three feet away from it," Magnolia said. She put on her own coat and stepped outside. Looking down Front Street, she saw

Cade trotting toward her pulling a sled behind him. Chantal was on the sled, bound up in a coat and blanket. A huge grin spread across her face which was red from the cold.

"Faster, Daddy, faster, faster!" she was calling.

"I'm not a horse, darlin', I'm a person," Cade called back.

"Cade McCall, what are you doing with that child out here in the frigid air? You need to get her somewhere warm," Magnolia said when they drew near.

"I'm not cold. I want to go on the sled," Chantal said.

"You heard her," Cade replied, his smile as broad as the one on the little girl's face. "She wants to go on the sled."

"All right, but not too much longer. You don't want her getting sick."

"*Grand mere's* making a pot of chicken soup," Cade said. "One more time up and back, and we'll go in. All right, sweetheart?" he added, turning toward Chantal.

"I like chicken soup," Chantal said.

"I do too, especially when I can have it with my best girl."

Magnolia watched Cade break into a trot again, then she went back inside.

"Is everything all right with Cade and Chantal?" Jeter asked as he helped her off with his coat.

"Oui, Zheeter, tout est magnifique. It is so heartwarming to watch the two of them together. "

"It is, isn't it? More than anything else, she has given him a reason for living."

Epilogue

Twin Creek Ranch, Howard County, Texas – 1927:

"BRANCH AND BOURBON," Owen Wister said, "I need it after this story. I had no idea the great Cade McCall was ever such a . . .a . . ."

"A bastard? I'll say it." Cade replied pouring a drink for both of them. "I don't know how I ever found such a friend as Jeter Willis. It's a wonder he didn't shoot me."

The two men were sitting in the swing on the front porch, rocking it gently back and forth with the slightest movement of their legs. In the west, the sinking sun had painted the sky crimson and gold.

"So, tell me, what happened to the Devil's Den?" Wister asked.

"Jeter took it back, fixed it up, made it even better than it had been and it became the Red House again."

"Did you own half of it?"

"Oh no." Cade laughed. "Jeter wasn't about to go down that road again. We traded his ownership in the freight company, for my ownership in the saloon, so that he became the sole owner. Pete Cahill, and the two girls who had worked for him all came back."

"What about the young girl? The one that came to stay with Magnolia to get away from the man who was after her?"

"Ah, yes, that would be Cetti. Well, Cetti, her sister Frankie, and Rosalie all came to work for Jeter except they took their birth names. They became Concetta, Florentina, and Antoinette."

"Did they stay in Dodge City?"

"Antoinette did. She and Maggie made the restaurant part of the Red House, the finest eating establishment in Southwest Kansas. I think Florentina married a lieutenant and left with him when Fort Dodge was closed. But Cetti, she saved her money and went to college. She became a teacher, and you'll never guess where she is today."

"No, where is she?"

"She married a congressman and she's in Washington D.C."

"It's too bad the story of Lola couldn't have had a happy ending, but I'm glad she was able to tell Jeter the truth about your card game in Caldwell."

"It was more for me than for him." Cade took another swallow of his drink before he continued. "You know, I would have gone to my grave thinking I'd lost the Red House for him."

"I'm glad he found out," Wister said, "but I'm glad he forgave you before he knew the truth."

"Yes, I've done a lot of things in my life, Dan," Cade said, using the name by which Owen Wister's friends addressed him. "I've met famous and powerful people, and I've been fortunate enough to make a lot of money.

But I count the long friendship I had with Jeter Willis as one of my greatest treasures. I miss him." Cade looked away to hide the tear that had formed in his eye.

THE END

A look at Diablo Double Cross by Robert Vaughan

Introducing Marcus Quinn and his raiders. Ex-Rebel out to take what they can get and then some. The war between the States is over, and Quinn's Raiders, the fiercest unit of guerrilla fighters in the South, are on their way to Texas to swing for their crimes. But no Yankee prison train can hold these boys for long.

Available from Wolfpack Publishing and Robert Vaughan.

About the Author

Robert Vaughan sold his first book when he was 19. That was 57 years and nearly 500 books ago. He wrote the novelization for the mini series *Andersonville*. Vaughan wrote, produced, and appeared in the History Channel documentary Vietnam Homecoming. His books have hit the NYT bestseller list seven times. He has won the Spur Award, the PORGIE Award (Best Paperback Original), the Western Fictioneers Lifetime Achievement Award, received the Readwest President's Award for Excellence in Western Fiction, is a member of the American Writers Hall of Fame and is a Pulitzer Prize nominee. Vaughn is also a retired army officer, helicopter pilot with three tours in Vietnam. And received the Distinguished Flying Cross, the Purple Heart, The Bronze Star with three oak leaf clusters, the Air Medal for valor with 35 oak leaf clusters, the Army Commendation Medal, the Meritorious Service Medal, and the Vietnamese Cross of Gallantry.

Find more great titles by Robert Vaughan and Wolfpack Publishing at http://wolfpackpublishing.com/robert-vaughan/